THE FORTUNES OF TEXAS

Follow the lives and loves of a complex family with a rich history and deep ties in the Lone Star State

FORTUNE'S SECRET CHILDREN

Six siblings discover they're actually part of the notorious Fortune family and move to Chatelaine, Texas, to claim their name...while uncovering shocking truths and life-changing surprises. Will their Fortunes turn—hopefully, for the better?

After the shock of an unexpected pregnancy subsides, Sabrina Fortune has one focus: giving her twins the best life possible. Problem is, that means co-parenting—and sparring—with equally opinionated Zane Baston. But with their lives so entangled, their hearts may not be far behind...

T0197855

Dear Reader,

Zane Baston and Sabrina Fortune are learning what to expect when they're expecting, and it's not what they expected at all. First on the list? That they're expecting in the first place! Zane has just finished raising his four brothers, for crying out loud. And the last thing Sabrina has thought about in, oh...ever...is having kids.

But here they are, trying to figure out how to work this co-parenting thing. Cue the disagreements about names and nursery themes and gender-specific toys. It's gonna be a long gestation.

Eventually, though, they realize that when it comes to starting a family, the most important thing is, well, family. They'll do whatever it takes to ensure their twins (yes, twins!) have the best of everything there is.

I had so much fun writing about Zane and Sabrina and the fabulous Fortune family. I hope you have as much fun reading about them.

All the best,

Elizabeth

NINE MONTHS TO A FORTUNE

ELIZABETH BEVARLY

THE FORTUNES OF TEXAS

Special thanks and acknowledgment are given to
Elizabeth Bevarly for her contribution to
The Fortunes of Texas: Fortune's Secret Children miniseries.

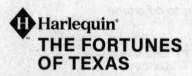

Harlequin®
THE FORTUNES OF TEXAS

Recycling programs
for this product may
not exist in your area.

ISBN-13: 978-1-335-99673-2

Nine Months to a Fortune

Copyright © 2024 by Harlequin Enterprises ULC

Harlequin Enterprises ULC
22 Adelaide St. West, 41st Floor
Toronto, Ontario M5H 4E3, Canada
www.Harlequin.com

Printed in Lithuania

MIX
Paper | Supporting
responsible forestry
FSC® C021394

Elizabeth Bevarly is the *New York Times* and *USA TODAY* bestselling author of more than eighty books. She has called home such exotic places as Puerto Rico and New Jersey but now lives outside her hometown of Louisville, Kentucky, with her husband and cat. When she's not writing or reading, she enjoys cooking, tending her kitchen garden and feeding the local wildlife. Visit her at elizabethbevarly.com for news and lots of fun stuff.

Books by Elizabeth Bevarly

The Fortunes of Texas: Fortune's Secret Children

Nine Months to a Fortune

Harlequin Special Edition

Seasons in Sudbury

Heir in a Year
Her Second-Chance Family

Lucky Stars

Be Careful What You Wish For
Her Good-Luck Charm
Secret under the Stars

Harlequin Desire

Taming the Prince
Taming the Beastly M.D.
Married to His Business
The Billionaire Gets His Way
My Fair Billionaire
Caught in the Billionaire's Embrace

Visit the Author Profile page
at Harlequin.com for more titles.

For David. Again. And Eli. Again.
Because how could I write about family
without both of you being there with me?
Love you guys.

Chapter One

Sabrina Fortune was panicking. And pacing. But mostly panicking.

Eyes fixed on the phone timer that was slowly—too slowly—ticking down the seconds, she carefully placed one foot in front of the other to make her way across her bedroom. It should have been an easy trek, considering she still didn't have her new place completely furnished, and the only obstacles in the room were the bed, dresser and slipper chair she'd brought from her much smaller condo in Dallas when she'd joined her family here in Chatelaine Hills. And all of those were pretty minimalist style, so it was all barely there to begin with.

She really did need to buy some furniture to fill in the currently very sparsely furnished luxe log cabin she'd been calling home for almost a month. Ever since her mother, Wendy—after discovering she was a long-lost member of the famous Fortune family—bought a ranch in Chatelaine, Texas, and convinced her six children to join her in living on it. Sabrina had been the last to arrive in the tiny lakefront town and was still getting acclimated to her job as the ranch accountant. But her mother and siblings already had a million plans for the place, including, but not limited to, a dairy business, some sheep, a petting zoo, which—Sabrina hoped, since it would help her out with the fiber arts therapy camp she herself wanted to start—might even include some goats and alpacas and llamas, and…and…

And where was she?

Right. Panicking. And pacing so anxiously that her steps were becoming even more erratic than her thoughts. *Anxious* and *erratic* weren't words people normally used to describe her. Sabrina Windham—no, Sabrina *Fortune*, she corrected herself, since her mother had also convinced all of the Windham children to change their last names, too—was normally the most forthright, most do-right, most upright…most up*tight*, some had said, though naturally she didn't agree with that—and she didn't like feeling anxious and erratic now. But it wasn't exactly surprising in light of the news she'd received that morning. News she still couldn't quite believe. Hence the pacing and the timer and the frazzled nerves. When she bumped her hip against the edge of her bed's footboard *again*, she decided to leave the bedroom and move out into the hallway, where she would have better room to pace some more.

She studied the timer on her phone as she stepped through the door. Three minutes and thirty-eight seconds to go. The instructions for the home pregnancy test she'd picked up at a convenience store on her way home from the doctor this morning said she would have results in five to ten minutes, but not to wait any longer than that or she might get a false positive result. No way did she want to risk a false positive result. She didn't even want a true positive result. But she hadn't wanted to be hasty, either, and check right at five minutes, just in case that wasn't quite enough time and might give a false negative when what she really wanted was a true negative, so eight minutes seemed like a good compromise, and—

Breathe, Sabrina, breathe.

She closed her eyes and inhaled deeply through her mouth, then exhaled slowly through her nose. She'd read somewhere that that was what you were supposed to do when you were panicking. And boy was she panicking.

With measured steps, she walked past the two bedrooms on the other side of her own master suite, past the guest bath and the small den she was gradually turning into a home office. Then she turned to pace back again. She'd honestly been wondering what she was going to do with all this extra space, since the six guesthouses lining Lake Chatelaine that had come with the ranch—and which were now being occupied by Sabrina and her five siblings—were, in her opinion, way too big for one person. But it was looking like Mother Nature might have an idea—at least for Sabrina's own not-so-crowded house. Biting her lip, she looked at her phone again.

One minute and seventeen seconds to go.

She couldn't be pregnant, she told herself for perhaps the hundredth time in a matter of hours. Especially not *twelve weeks* pregnant. She didn't care what her gynecologist had told her that morning. There was simply no way Sabrina Fortune could have gotten knocked up. She'd only had sex one time in the last three years—which, okay, had been twelve weeks ago—and they'd used protection. Correctly, too, if memory served, though, admittedly, in the heat of the moment—and there had been *a lot* of heated moments that night— things, and condoms, could go awry. But she'd had irregular periods ever since getting her first when she was twelve. Just because she'd missed the last two, that didn't mean she was pregnant...

Twenty-two seconds to go.

She'd left the test in the master bathroom because she hadn't wanted to be tempted to watch the results as they materialized. They weren't going to materialize— at least not in the positive. Because she wasn't pregnant. She couldn't be.

Nine...eight...seven...six...

Hastily, Sabrina made her way back to the other end of the hall, into her bedroom and the en suite bath. Her phone's timer sounded just as she stepped over the threshold, a series of gentle beeps that erupted in her ears like the banging of a fireworks finale. The little plastic test tray was sitting on the edge of the sink where she'd left it, looking completely innocuous in the soft white light reflecting off the pale blue walls. At least, it looked innocuous until she drew close enough to see the results.

A perfect pink plus sign. Sabrina Fortune was indeed pregnant.

Strangely, upon seeing her own personal confirmation of what her doctor had already told her—and what she had been so determined to mire herself in denial about until she could prove it to herself—her anxiety evaporated, to be replaced by... Something else. She wasn't sure what. She only knew she wasn't panicking anymore. The sight of that little plus sign was just so…surreal. Everything suddenly seemed to shift, as if the floor beneath her tilted, and she tumbled into another world that looked like the one she was used to, but didn't feel like the same place at all. She might as well have been the only person who even existed in this strange new world.

Well, her and the life that was growing inside her.

Without thinking, she splayed her hand open over her belly, as if trying to find some kind of bodily proof, too, of what the test had just told her. But nothing felt different. She wondered how long it would be before anyone would be able to tell.

She shoved her phone into the pocket of the beige shirtwaist she'd donned that morning—since she'd planned to go to work after seeing her doctor—and ran restless fingers through her pale blond bangs.

Gingerly, she picked up the test tray, cradling it in her palm as if it were a sacred jewel. Then she went back down the hall to her home office to sit down at her desk. She pushed aside the handwritten figures from the ranch's previous accountant that she'd been trying to decipher yesterday—way back when she thought she was only seeing her gynecologist today to make sure this latest double-period-skipping wasn't something more concerning—and set the sliver of plastic at the center of her desk. Then she withdrew her phone again and snapped a quick photo. The little pink plus sign would fade soon, and the way she felt now, she might need evidence to convince herself later of what she still didn't quite want to believe.

She was pregnant. Twelve weeks. Almost to the day. She knew that, because it had been twelve weeks since she attended a glitzy fundraiser for a children's rodeo right here in Chatelaine, at the posh Chatelaine Hills Hotel and Resort. May 30. She'd never forget that date. Now it was September 2. How could it be more than three months since she met Zane Baston, the wealthy rancher with the dreamy green eyes who also lived right here in Chatelaine. Talk about tall, dark and handsome. Zane was all those things and then some. From the moment their gazes connected, something white hot had arced through the air between them, setting fire to a place inside her that had been cold for too long. As if they were two halves of a whole that had been separated for eons and were finally being pulled back together again. And, wow, had the two of them been pulled together that night. There were parts of Sabrina that were still sizzling, three months later. She'd never met a man like him.

And now that man was trying to pull a land grab of a small parcel of lakefront property that abutted the Fortune Ranch. A parcel of land Sabrina had already purchased and had big plans for but hadn't been able to claim yet because Zane Baston had some of his cronies at town hall doing everything they could to negate the sale so that he could claim the land for himself. Sabrina could scarcely believe her property nemesis was the same man she met that night three months ago. Except he thought he was dealing with Sabrina Fortune, she knew, and not the Sabrina Windham he'd met that night.

She closed her eyes again, but this time it was to envision what she'd written off twelve weeks ago as just one of those things, like the old song said. She'd never planned on seeing Zane again after that night, because she knew she'd be returning to Dallas in the morning. The only reason she'd come to the fundraiser in the first place was to check out the little town her mother had been raving about for months. Then again, now that she thought about it, being sure she'd never see Zane again might have been why she'd let things go too far that night.

She still couldn't believe they'd ended up in bed together. Sabrina was never that impetuous. Never that spontaneous. Of the six Fortune siblings, she'd always been The Cautious One. Especially after—

Well, suffice to say that for the last ten years, Sabrina had made it an extra fine point to live her life carefully. Thoughtfully. Deliberately. She seldom dated, and what few relationships—if she could even call them that—she had managed to develop over the years had all ended quickly when both she and her potential partner realized how hard it was for her to open herself up to an emotional commitment. She'd learned her lesson there.

Even so, she had to tell Zane he was going to be a father. He had the right to know. Then he could do with the knowledge what he would. Just how she was supposed to tell him, though?

She inhaled another deep breath and released it slowly. There was just one thing to do. The thing Sabrina had done her entire life when it came to times of turmoil. She was going to have to assemble her sisters.

"So I guess you're all wondering why I've called you here tonight," Sabrina said some hours later after pouring glasses of wine for her twin sister, Dahlia, and her older sister Jade.

She'd changed into her usual nightwear of pajama pants—these pinstriped in pink and pale yellow—and a tunic the color of buttercups. Her pale blond hair was bound at her nape in a loose ponytail, much like her sister Dahlia's, but that was about where the fraternal twins' similarities ended. Where they were both tall, Dahlia had curves that lanky Sabrina could only dream about, every last one of them evident in Dahlia's work-about-the-ranch blue jeans and white button-up shirt. Her blond hair was a shade lighter than Sabrina's, and her blue eyes were dark and expressive where Sabrina liked to think she kept her own thoughts to herself. Jade's hair was long, too, but was dark brown and fell loose around her shoulders. Her own style was more conservative as well, and hadn't changed much over the years, her blue jeans and T-shirt much like what she wore when they were in high school.

Really, all six of the Fortune siblings had features that ran the gamut. Some were dark, some fair, some were in between. Yet they somehow all managed to resemble both their mother, Wendy, and their father, Casper.

Jade and Dahlia accepted the wine from Sabrina gratefully, and each enjoyed a generous sip after giving her their thanks. Looked like they'd both had One of

Those Days, too. But she'd also bet dollars to doughnuts those days were nothing compared to her own.

"You sound like you're going to accuse us of murder," Jade said from her seat on Sabrina's sofa.

Her living room, too, was still sparsely furnished, the delicate curves and pale colors of her furniture looking overwhelmed by the soaring beams and honey-gold logs of the living room. She was definitely going to have to do some furniture shopping soon.

"So who died?" Dahlia asked.

Sabrina sighed. "My sense of self."

"Well, that doesn't sound good," Dahlia replied.

"Have a sip of wine and tell us what's going on," Jade told her.

Sabrina looked down at her glass, into which she'd poured a generous serving of pomegranate juice. "It's not wine," she told them. "It's juice."

"Wow, you really have lost your sense of self," Dahlia said with a chuckle.

"Indeed," Jade concurred. "Explain yourself."

Sabrina smiled at her sisters in spite of the turmoil cartwheeling through her. Usually, these conclaves with her sisters weren't about anything too major. A lot of times, it was just girls having fun. Tonight, though, she needed help sorting things out. But how was she supposed to explain any of this to Dahlia and Jade when she didn't understand it herself?

In an effort to stall, she asked her sisters, "Hey, how's Hope doing? Have either of you spoken to her lately?"

Hope was a woman who Dahlia and their brother Ridge had discovered in his barn late one night last month with a baby in her arms, a wound on her head, and absolutely no memory of who she was or how she'd gotten there. Ridge had taken her in, along with baby Evie, but the last Sabrina had heard, they hadn't made any headway in discovering her identity or history. They didn't even know if her name was truly Hope.

"She's doing well physically," Dahlia said. "I talked to them yesterday. The doctor gave her and Evie both a clean bill of health and told Hope that her memory should return in time. Nothing seems to be jarring any recollections, though."

Sabrina couldn't imagine what it must be like to have no inkling of who you were. And to have a baby to care for on top of that. She was just happy Hope and Evie had found their way to a place where they'd be safe. Her youngest brother, Ridge, was just about the most decent human being Sabrina knew.

"But enough about Hope," Jade said. "What's happening with you? Why are we here?"

When Sabrina didn't reply right away, Dahlia and Jade grew visibly concerned.

"You okay, sis?" Dahlia asked.

Sabrina shook her head. "Not really. I'm…"

"What?" Jade demanded.

Just tell them, Sabrina instructed herself. "I'm…I'm pregnant."

She might as well have just told her sisters she had indeed murdered someone, so incredulous were their expressions.

"What?" Jade echoed, with even more concern this time.

"How?" Dahlia wanted to know. "I mean, I know *how.* But *who?*"

So Sabrina sat down and told them everything. How she'd succumbed so quickly to her attraction to Zane that night. How she wished she could put it down to something like too many glasses of wine or the magic of the evening or anything else. But she'd only had a couple of glasses, and the evening had been just like any other glitzy fundraiser of the dozens she'd attended as an accountant for a Dallas nonprofit. There really had been nothing magical about that night.

Except for Zane. And his dreamy green eyes. Eyes that had been completely fixed on her face the minute she took her assigned seat across from him at the dinner table.

She bit back a sigh at the memories of the gorgeous man with amazing eyes and chiseled cheekbones who introduced himself with a laid-back, velvety *Hey, there, I'm Zane.* She'd nearly melted into a puddle under the table when he'd reached out a hand to shake hers. A jolt of something hot and electric had shot through her whole body, and she'd barely been able to remember her own name. When she hadn't given it to him right away, he'd picked up the place card above her dinner plate and turned it toward himself. *Sabrina Windham,* he'd purred in that luscious baritone—she hadn't yet changed her last name to Fortune. *I am* very *pleased to make your acquaintance.* The next thing she knew, they were sharing hot, moon-drenched kisses in the rose garden gazebo, And then… Oh, *and then.* Her body grew

hot all over again just thinking about their night of un-
inhibited lovemaking back at his ranch…

"I've actually met Zane Baston a time or two," Jade
said when Sabrina finished her account. "And you're
right. He's pretty hot. Not so hot that I'd have a one-night
stand with him…" she added meaningfully.

"We used a condom," Sabrina assured them. "I did
mention we used a condom, right? Correctly, too."

Then again, it had gotten pretty intense pretty fast
that night. Something else she'd confessed to her sisters. Amazing. That was what it had been. Every woman
should have a night like that at least once in her life.
But when Sabrina had opened her eyes the following
morning, reality had come crashing back down around
her. Without thinking, she'd dressed and collected her
things while Zane was still asleep, then called for a
rideshare, which had thankfully come quickly. She'd
returned to the hotel, packed her bags, checked out and
headed home, confident that she would never see Zane
again. Even if, someplace deep inside her, she'd been
wishing the whole time that there was some way she
could stay in Chatelaine with him for— Well. For a
while longer, at least.

"Which was maybe why I finally let Mom talk me
into moving here to Chatelaine with the rest of you
guys," she admitted to her sisters now.

"Oh, come on," Jade said. "You knew you'd miss us
if you didn't. We've always been a close family, and
Dad's death and Mom's learning about being a Fortune
has only made us tighter."

This was certainly true. Her family had always been

close. But they'd grown closer in the wake of their father's death from pancreatic cancer the previous year. It had happened so suddenly after all. Only weeks between his diagnosis and his funeral because, true to Casper Windham form, his workaholic tendencies had made him ignore his symptoms until it was too late. After that, family had come to mean more to the surviving Windhams—now Fortunes—than ever before.

"Truer words, big sister," Dahlia agreed. "In times of trouble, family stands strong, whether their name is Windham or Fortune or… Hey, are you going to give the baby Zane's last name, or will it be a Fortune, too?"

Sabrina uttered a helpless sound. "I have no idea. I haven't even told him yet. I haven't even seen him since moving to Chatelaine. I've been doing everything I can to avoid him because he and I are vying over that piece of land I need for the fiber arts grief camp I want to start."

"Oh, wow, I forgot about that," Jade said.

"Yeah, that does muddy things up a bit," Dahlia agreed.

"Especially since he doesn't realize it's the woman he met at the fundraiser who he's at odds with. That woman was named Sabrina Windham. He thinks he's trying to take the land from someone named Sabrina Fortune." She sighed. "But even without all that, I still have no idea how I feel about that night."

She was even less sure of how Zane would react when she saw her again. He hadn't exactly gone out of his way to contact her, either, after her return to Dallas. But Chatelaine was the very definition of small town.

She was bound to see him eventually. He was bound to see her. And when he learned that she was pregnant, he'd put two and two together pretty quickly.

Then Sabrina remembered something else. She remembered how Zane told her that night about losing his parents when he was a teenager and raising his four younger brothers alone. Any man who would assume the care and feeding of four young boys when he wasn't that far from boyhood himself was a man who would always do the right thing. Once Zane found out he was going to become a father, he'd want to be a part of that child's life. The two of them could very well be connected forever.

"You have to tell him, Sabrina," Jade said. "He has a right to know he's going to be a father."

Dahlia nodded in agreement. "It'll be okay. Life is full of surprises. Stuff happens. It's a lesson everyone needs to learn."

"This is true," Jade said. "God knows all of us have had to learn it over the last year."

Everything her sisters said was what Sabrina had been telling herself all afternoon. Especially the part about life lessons. It felt like a lifetime had passed since their father's death and Wendy's discovery that the mother she'd always known wasn't actually her mother and that she had a dying grandfather who was leaving her an honest-to-God castle here in Chatelaine. She had wanted desperately to leave their hometown of Cactus Grove after her husband's death, and neither Sabrina nor her siblings had really felt any major ties to the place. Their father hadn't always been an easy man to love, having held his business closer than he had his family. It hadn't taken long for them to capitulate to their mother's wishes for both the name change and the move because Wendy had always done her best by all of them.

"I still can't believe Sabrina met Zane here in Chatelaine before we even moved here," Dahlia said.

"I know, right?" Jade replied. "What are the odds? We barely knew Chatelaine existed until we got here."

"Well, Sabrina knew," Dahlia said with a sly smile. "She had the greatest sex of her life here after all."

"Very funny," Sabrina retorted.

"Hey, your words, sis, not mine."

Actually, Sabrina had told them it was the most *amazing* sex. Though why she had let that little nugget slip, she had no idea. Pregnancy hormones, she told herself now. She'd heard they could make a woman feel a little, um, different.

"Anyway," Dahlia continued, "it's kind of unreal that Sabrina would have a one-night stand in some out-of-the-way town and wind up preggers."

"Hey," Sabrina retorted, "at least I didn't wake up in Vegas with no memory of the night before married to my nemesis since kindergarten. Unlike *some* people."

"Yeah, but I'm not The Cautious One," Dahlia reminded her. She smiled. "Besides. Waking up next to Rawlston that morning ended up turning out pretty well for me."

"I'm just surprised Sabrina had a one-night stand at all," Jade interjected. "Not after what happened with Pres—"

Here she halted, her expression indicating how sorry

she was to have said what she did. Not the part about the one-night stand, but the words that came after that were way too close to broaching a subject no one in the family ever talked about. Sabrina's marriage to Preston Stallard. One that had ended before it could even begin. One she simply did not allow anyone—including herself—to talk about. Because it was just too painful.

"Anyway," Sabrina said, throwing each of her sisters a warning look, "what happened happened, and now I have to figure out what to do next."

"You haven't heard a word from Zane since that night?" Jade asked.

"Not as Sabrina Windham," Sabrina said. "And all the stuff with the land grab is going through our attorneys and Realtors."

She had been both relieved and disappointed not to hear from Zane after their night together. Then again, she hadn't contacted him, either. Maybe they'd both realized the morning after that it was just one of those things. For all Sabrina knew, that kind of thing happened to Zane all the time. She was probably just one of dozens of women he'd spent the night with this year alone.

"He needs to know," Dahlia said, echoing her earlier statement. "You have to tell him. Then he can make his own decision about what he wants to do."

"What is it *you* want to do, Sabrina?" Jade asked pointedly.

Surprisingly, it was the first time since realizing she was pregnant that she gave that some thought. She'd never really considered having children. First because she was too young. She and Preston had told themselves they had plenty of time. Then, after his death, she'd been certain there would never be anyone special in her life again to think about having children with. But she was thirty-two years old now. This baby might be her only chance to become a mother. Did she *want* to be a mother? Was she in a position to provide for a child? Was she ready to set aside her own wants and needs to put another human being first? Would she even be a good mom?

She was surprised to realize that all of those questions had the same answer. *Yes*.

She looked at her sisters and found them gazing back at her with much expectation.

So she told them, "I'm keeping the baby. And I'll find Zane tomorrow and tell him he's going to be a father. Then he and I can go from there." She smiled at each of her sisters in turn and added, "Also, I think the two of you are going to be the coolest aunties ever."

Chapter Two

Zane Baston was sitting in the middle of the floor in his home office doing his best to figure out how to fit the peg of tent pole A into the hole of tent pole B—no easy feat when he hadn't even located tent pole B—when he heard the doorbell ring downstairs.

It was odd for anyone to come calling at the house now that three of his younger brothers were living on their respective college campuses, and the fourth was headed that way soon. So Zane ignored the summons. It was probably someone who'd likewise ignored the No Soliciting sign on the driveway gate he never bothered to close, and he knew his housekeeper, Astrid, would take care of whoever it was. Nobody ever wanted to mess with a Nordic Valkyrie old enough to be their grandma but sturdy enough to kick their butts to Asgard and back. And he really did need to find the pieces to the tent—and figure out how to assemble them all—before he left on his trip at the end of the month.

It had been his dream when he was a teenager to travel around the world for a year after he graduated from college. But within months of his receiving his degree, he and his brothers lost their parents when the elder Bastons' private plane went down. At twenty-three, Zane took on the role of raising his four little brothers, who hadn't even been teenagers when their parents died. Now three of those little boys had left the nest for college, and the fourth had one foot out the door. Before leaving, though, they'd pooled money from part-time jobs and trust funds so they could make Zane's trip happen—their way of saying thanks for all the sacrifices he'd made for them. For the better part of the year ahead, Zane was going to be able to visit all the places he'd only fantasized about before.

Boom. Dream come true. One item ticked off his bucket list.

It was a trip he would have been over the moon about ten years ago, when nothing had seemed more thrilling or important to him than seeing the world. But he kind of had mixed feelings about it now. A decade brought a lot of changes to a man's life. But his brothers had insisted that since the last of them was off to college, Zane *had* to go. Not only had they already worked out the logistics for the care of the ranch with his foreman, Mateo—who was also delighted Zane was going to finally be able to enjoy his dream trip of a lifetime—but the four boys had also pooled *a lot* of their financial resources to make sure he could. So, in a matter of weeks, Zane was off on the first leg.

Sydney, Australia, ready or not, here I come.

He was even wearing one of those half-flipped-up hats that his youngest brother, Cody, had found somewhere online and insisted Zane take with him. An Akubra hat, he'd called it. Zane just hoped they really wore these things Down Under. For now, though, he was only wearing it around the house and only to appease the kid.

"Mr. Baston?"

He looked up to see Astrid standing in the door-way of the office whose Spanish Colonial decor hadn't changed one whit since his parents' deaths. Dark wood paneling rose halfway up the creamy walls, interrupted by bookcases filled with family memorabilia and knick-knacks, potted cacti and, oh, yeah, books. The big, or-nate mahogany desk was complemented by a pair of coffee-colored leather chairs, and a massive wool rug patterned in Mexican geometrics spanned the floor. Zane had always loved playing in here when he was a boy while his father did the ranch paperwork. He could still feel the scratch of the old rug under his knees as he pushed his Hot Wheels along the pattern, pretend-ing the jagged lines were roads. Hell, here he was still, sitting on the same rug.

Then again, his folks hadn't really changed any part of Night Heron Ranch at all from when his grandparents owned it. And his grandparents probably hadn't changed anything much from when his great-grandparents first settled here in the early 1900s. The big adobe Spanish Colonial with the terra-cotta tile roof looked, inside and out, like something from a fabulous forties film about the taming of the Wild West. He loved this place with all his heart. It had been perfect for growing a family, and it felt strangely empty already now that the last of his brothers was on his way out.

As he always did whenever Astrid called him *Mr.*

Baston, he replied, "You can call me Zane, Astrid. Everyone does."

And as she had always done when she replied, she reiterated, "Mr. Baston, there's a woman downstairs who says she needs to speak to you. I told her you were busy and asked her to make an appointment for later, but she insists she needs to speak to you today, about something very important."

Okay, that was weird. Whatever business Zane had to conduct off the ranch, he conducted in Chatelaine proper over a cup of coffee and a cattleman's breakfast at the Cowgirl Café. And he'd made it a practice a long time ago to never bring women home with him since the house had always been full of impressionable kids. In fact, he'd only brought one woman here to the ranch—and only one time—but that was because all the boys were away that weekend, and the woman in question had been like none he'd ever met before. He still grew warm inside thinking about her and the way they'd come together that night. But she'd disappeared without a trace before he woke up the next morning, never to be seen again.

"She said to tell you her name is Sabrina Windham," Astrid told him.

Until today.

A tidal wave of heat tsunamied through Zane's belly just hearing her name again. He hadn't seen Sabrina for months. Not since that incredible night at the end of May.

Wow. Speak of the devil. With a blue dress on. Because he was still haunted by the vision of her that night at the fundraiser, when he'd glanced away from a conversation about freemartins that was going on way too long to see the most incredible woman he'd ever seen sitting down on the other side of his table. As if she'd felt his gaze on her, she'd looked right at him, and for one indescribable moment, the whole world seemed to slip away. The next thing he knew, they were talking like they'd known each other for years. After dinner, there had been dancing, so dance they did. Right out onto a terrace adjacent to the ballroom, across the terrace to the garden, down the garden path to a secluded passage of roses that had smelled heavenly, straight to a gazebo where Zane had kissed her. And kissed her. And kissed her. Then he was inviting her back to his ranch for a nightcap, and she was saying yes, and then they were at his ranch, ignoring the nightcap because he started kissing her again the minute they got through the door, and then they were in his bedroom, and then…

Oh, man. And *then*.

"Uh, go ahead and show her up," he told Astrid.

He'd never thought he'd see Sabrina again. They hadn't exchanged phone numbers that night, so he'd had no way to contact her after the fact. He'd tried to find her online, but what few social media accounts he'd found for her had all been set to private. He'd thought about trying to message her on one of them anyway, but the fact that she took off literally under cover of darkness without even saying goodbye or leaving a note had been a pretty good indication she hadn't wanted to see him again. As much as he'd hated to do it, he'd chalked up their time together as just one of those things. Hell, he'd had one-night hookups in the past that had been easy enough to move past. Why should Sabrina Windham be any different?

But Sabrina Windham *had* been different. As much as he'd tried to forget her, he still found himself thinking about her from time to time. How gorgeous she'd been dressed in that sleek sapphire dress the same color as her eyes. How silky her hair had been, sifting through his fingers when he tugged free the comb holding it in place. How soft her skin had been when he'd pulled her naked body against his. That sweet, arousing little sound she made when he touched the heated, damp core of her. How he'd come apart at the seams when the two of them climaxed together. How…uh…um…

Anyway, he did still think about that night occasionally. But, hey, it had only been a few months. He knew he'd get over her eventually. Probably.

But what the hell was she doing here?

As if in answer to his unspoken question, she appeared in the doorway where Astrid had stood a moment ago, looking even more beautiful than he remembered. She was wearing blue again, but this dress was the pale blue of a summer sky. Her hair was up again, too, however today, it was neatly wound into a tidy topknot, with not a single strand out of place. She was clinging to a small purse slung over her shoulder, so tightly that she might as well have been carrying the nuclear launch codes in it.

"Hi," she said, so softly he almost didn't hear her. She smiled in a way that was at once anxious and arousing. With a bit more fortitude, she added, "Remember me?"

He smiled back. "Hell, yes, I remember you."

Without thinking, he took a few steps across the room, then stopped when he realized the reason he was doing it was to kiss her. As if that were the most natural thing in the world for him to do, even after not seeing her for months. Even after spending only a single night together, one that ended with her leaving without saying goodbye. One where, for a little while, at least, it had felt as if the two of them belonged together.

Her eyes widened a bit when he started to move toward her, but she didn't look like she wanted to retreat. He marveled again that an entire season had come and gone since he last saw her. At the moment, it felt like no time had passed at all. As if that very morning, he'd awakened beside her in the hazy light of a new day and kissed her hello, then shared breakfast with her before setting about his day, with no reason to think he wouldn't see her again when it was time to go home that evening.

Why would he feel like that? He hadn't awakened beside her in his bed the morning after they made love, and he hadn't kissed her hello that day. Hell, he hadn't even kissed her goodbye.

What was she doing here?

"It's good to see you," he said.

Yeah, it was a cliché, but it was true. It was good to see Sabrina again. Surprisingly good. A ribbon of warmth wound through him as she took a few steps forward as well. But she stopped when a good five feet still separated them.

"It's good to see you, too," she told him. She looked

at some point just above him. "Interesting headgear for a Texas rancher."

He was confused for a moment, then remembered the Akubra hat. "A gift from my youngest brother, Cody," he said.

She smiled. "And how are your brothers?" she asked. "There are four of them, right? And the youngest one is off to college soon, if I remember correctly."

He was delighted that she did in fact remember correctly. "Yeah, Cody starts classes next week. Something for which I am extremely grateful, because he'd been threatening to drop out of high school for months and run off with his girlfriend to join the rodeo. The twins are both in San Antonio, since although they wanted to be separated, they didn't want to be separated, if you get my drift."

Sabrina laughed. "As a twin myself, I totally do."

Zane laughed, too. "That's right. I forgot you have a twin sister." He made a face. "Sorry, don't remember her name."

"Dahlia."

"Right. Like the flower."

"My sister Jade is also a twin, to my brother Nash. Fraternal, all of us."

"So are my brothers," Zane said with a smile. "Anyway, Shane is at Trinity, and Levi is at Texas A&M–San Antonio. And the oldest, Wyatt, is a junior at Baylor."

"Aren't you the oldest brother?" she asked with a smile.

Zane smiled back. "Yeah, I guess technically I am. But I've felt more like their parent since our folks have been gone." He remembered telling her the night of the fundraiser about raising his brothers. What he didn't remember was why he'd told her, since he didn't normally share that right off the bat with women. Something about Sabrina, though, had made him more forthcoming than usual.

She shook her head. "Four college tuitions at once. That can't be easy."

Zane waved a hand. "Nah, it's all good. My parents put college funds in place for all of us as soon as we were born. Then all four of my brothers ended up with full-ride or near full-ride scholarships. Smart as whips, all of them, and way more involved in the community than I was at their age." He smiled a little sheepishly. "They ended up pooling their college funds and the money they made from part-time jobs they got in high school to fund my trip."

Sabrina looked confused. "What trip?"

Oh, yeah. He hadn't told her that part the night of the fundraiser. They'd sorta gotten sidetracked by, um, other stuff.

"I'm leaving at the end of the month to spend a year traveling around the world. It was supposed to happen after I graduated from college—I spent years as a teenager planning it—but I had to cancel after our parents' deaths. Now that my brothers are all heading off on their own, they wanted to treat me to say thanks for the last ten years."

Now Sabrina looked a little panicky. Why would she look panicky? He was the one who was about to leave everything that was familiar for a year to go thousands of miles away.

"Wow," she finally said. A little panicky. "That's amazingly generous of them."

He shrugged. "When they told me about the trip, they said it wasn't near enough to pay me back for everything I'd done for them."

Although she still looked anxious about something, she smiled. "Those boys were raised right."

"Yeah, well, joke's on them, 'cause I got more out of raising them than they got out of being raised. They're all headed back to their respective campuses in a couple days, so we had our official send-off last night. Shane and Levi chipped in on this tent I need to figure out, and Wyatt gave me a compass because he's so sure I'll get lost somewhere along the way. Such a comedian, that one."

Gingerly, he removed the hat, then tossed it toward a nearby rack, where it landed perfectly between a leather bridle that needed repair and his favorite Stetson. Then he looked at Sabrina again.

"But yeah. Cody got me the hat because the trip starts in Sydney."

She nodded. "And you're leaving at the end of this month?"

He nodded back. "Yep."

"And you're going to be gone for a year?" Why did she look so worried when she asked that?

"Leaving the thirtieth," he told her. "Though I won't arrive in Sydney until October second. International dateline and all that."

"Guess when you're going to be gone a whole year, a couple days is just a drop in the bucket."

He nodded and realized he had no idea what to say in response. So he blurted out the question that had come to mind the second Astrid mentioned her name.

"Sabrina, what are you doing here?"

Now she was back to looking panicked.

"I mean, don't get me wrong," he hurried to add. "It really is good to see you, but…" He expelled a restless sound and reminded her, "The last time we saw each other…the only time we saw each other—" he made himself clarify "—you kind of left without warning, and it's not like you tried to get in touch afterward."

"I know," she said. "And I'm sorry about that, Zane. I truly am. I just… That night—" She halted, inhaled a deep breath and tried again. "I've never done anything like that before. Ever. I'm just not the type of person who can meet someone and hop into bed with them. I'm usually super careful and wary and…" She shifted her weight restlessly from one foot to the other and back again. "There are six kids in my family, and I've always been called 'The Cautious One.' Even when we were little kids, I looked before I leaped. No tree climbing, no eating dirt, no little white lies, no wandering off. I was way too careful. About everything."

Zane found this surprising. He'd immediately formed an impression of Sabrina as breezy and lighthearted, without a care in the world. No way could he see her as *cautious*.

She tried again. "After what happened between us, I didn't know what to do. That night was just so…"

He grinned at that. "Yeah, it was."

She chuckled, but the sound was nervous and, he had to admit, a little cautious.

"That night was wonderful," she assured him. "But afterward…" She blew out another errant breath. "I didn't know where we could go from there. My life was in Dallas then, yours was here. There was no reason to think our paths would ever cross again."

"So then…why are they crossing now?"

The gaze that had been so focused on his darted away. "I live in Chatelaine now," she told him.

The warmth that had been spiraling through him since her appearance pooled in the center of his chest and exploded. "Since when?"

"For about a month."

Now the heat dropped right to the pit of his belly. And not in a good way. She'd been here for a month but was only now contacting him? Why the delay? And what made her come now?

"And what's brought you to Chatelaine, Sabrina Windham?" he asked. Since it clearly hadn't been him, no matter how much he wished it had been. Had it been him, she would have come knocking at his door long before today.

"Actually, I'm not Sabrina Windham anymore," she replied, skirting the question. "I just told your housekeeper that so you'd recognize me. My name last name is Fortune now."

Zane's eyebrows shot up to his hairline. Naturally, he'd heard about how a whole new branch of the famous Fortune family had moved to Chatelaine earlier this year to join the ones who already lived here—

everyone in town had heard. He'd even met a couple of them in passing. But he'd so been busy with ranch work and getting Cody off to college, he hadn't paid the newcomers much mind. He certainly hadn't heard about a Sabrina For—

Oh, crap. Yes, he had. His Realtor and lawyer were currently wrangling with hers over a piece of land they both wanted. *That* must be why she'd come to the house today.

Then another thought struck him. If Sabrina had gone from being a Windham to being a Fortune, that must mean—

"You got *married*?" he exclaimed.

Now she looked panicked again, even more so than before. "No!" she quickly assured him. "God, no. I'm not married. I'm never getting married again."

"Married *again*?"

Before he could ask her to elaborate on that, she hurried on. "Long story, but my mom found out she was a Fortune after my dad's death last year, and she changed her name to embrace her new family. She asked all of us kids to change our names, too, since we're also official Fortunes. So now I'm Sabrina Fortune. *Single* Sabrina Fortune," she said adamantly.

Zane was surprised by the depth of the relief that wound through him to realize she was still unattached. He'd think about why later. He'd think about the *married again* part later, too. Not to mention the land-wrangling. But first things first.

"I mean, in my heart, I'll always be at least a bit of a Windham," Sabrina said. "Not all of us kids were super eager to do the name change. Especially since a new name doesn't change who you are."

"If the name is Fortune," Zane said, "and it's here in Texas, it totally changes who you are."

"Really?"

He grinned. "Oh, yeah. Might as well be European royalty."

Sabrina laughed. "Oh, right. Princess Sabrina, that's me."

"I don't know," he murmured. "You sure looked like a princess that night at the fundraiser."

Her cheeks stained with pink, and she glanced down at the floor. But she said nothing.

Quietly, he added, "Not to mention I kinda felt like Cinderella ran back to the pumpkin patch when I woke up alone the next morning."

She had the decency to look embarrassed by that. She opened her mouth to say something, but he held up a hand to stop her.

"You don't owe me an apology," he said. "We didn't make any promises to each other that night."

She looked like she wanted to object, but she backtracked, "If the name change makes my mother happy, and since all my brothers and sisters are on board with it…" She shrugged. "I love my family. Doesn't matter what our name is."

"Family is numero uno in these parts," Zane agreed.

"I don't know what I'd do without mine," she said. "But I didn't come here to tell you about my family."

Here it comes, Zane thought. She was going to give him an earful him about the land they both wanted.

But instead of lighting into him, she took a few more steps forward, opening her purse as she drew nearer. She withdrew her phone, punched in her code, did some scrolling, enlarged a photo she found in her collection and silently thrust it toward him. Her expression when she looked at him now was a mix of a million different emotions, none of which he could quite identify.

Warily, he took the phone from her and looked at the photo she'd chosen. It was of a small plastic tray, one of those medical testing kinds like a person used for a home diagnosis. One opening showing a very clear pink plus sign. He'd never seen a home pregnancy test in person, but this was sure what he figured they looked like. Either that, or Sabrina had some kind of contagious something or other, and she was telling him he had it now, too. Heat swelled in his belly again. One way or another, he knew, his life was about to change.

With even more trepidation than before, he asked softly, "What exactly am I looking at, Sabrina?"

"I was afraid the result would disappear after I took the test, so I snapped a photo. I knew I'd need to keep convincing myself after the fact."

His heart hammered hard in his chest. "Convince yourself of what?"

She inhaled an even deeper breath than before and released it even more slowly. "I'm pregnant, Zane. And you…you're the father. That's why I'm here. To tell you that. Because you deserve to know."

It took a few seconds for that to sink in. Because time just sorta stopped for a bit. His heart rate doubled, the heat in his belly spread to every pore in his body and his breath quickened.

Yep, he'd been right. His life was definitely about to change.

Chapter Three

If Sabrina could have chosen any superpower in the world at that moment, she would have chosen the ability to read minds. Because she could no more tell what Zane was thinking after her announcement than she could have made the Earth move in the opposite direction like Superman.

He was even more handsome than she recalled. The night of the fundraiser, he'd been dressed in a dark suit and crisp white shirt with a bolo tie, his dark hair cut short and his cheeks cleanly shaven. His hair was longer now, ruggedly tousled, and he looked as if he'd skipped a few days with the razor. He was dressed now in battered jeans and a faded blue work shirt, an outfit that made him seem earthy and affable. His green eyes, though, were exactly as she remembered, thickly lashed and the color of sage, as clear and deep as an ocean.

His gaze kept ricocheting from the phone in his hand to her face, as if he couldn't quite work out what he was looking at. Sabrina sympathized. She'd spent pretty much the entire day after taking the test doing exactly the same thing. She knew she had the advantage of a day and a half to accustom herself to her condition. Zane had barely had a second and a half. She understood it was going to take some time for him to figure out what he was feeling.

Except that it…didn't. Because he suddenly smiled as if he'd just won a billion-dollar lottery. Then he let out a whoop of delight and crossed what little distance separated them to pull Sabrina into a hug. Her breath caught as he swept her off her feet and spun her around a few times before setting her back on the floor. He didn't release her, though, only kept his arms roped loosely around her waist. Which she told herself should feel intrusive. But it didn't. It actually felt kind of nice. The expression on his face now, though, was clearly ecstatic. She'd never seen a human being look so happy.

"I'm going to be a *father*?" he asked.

The question was clearly rhetorical, since she'd already told him she was pregnant.

"A real, live, honest-to-God father?" he repeated.

Sabrina couldn't find her voice for some reason—probably because she was still trying to identify that ripple of unidentifiable something curling through her—so she only nodded. His reaction was just so surprising. She'd been afraid that, at best, he would have been stoic and pragmatic and accepting. And that, at worst, he'd be angry and contrary and tell her she was on her own. The last thing she had thought he would be was delighted.

He seemed to understand her confusion because his smile gentled. But he still didn't release her. And, strangely, Sabrina didn't mind that at all.

"You thought I'd be mad," he said.

She nodded again. "Kind of. Even more so now that

you've told me you're about to go on a dream trip around the world for a year. And you can still go," she hurried to reassure him. "You don't have to put your life on hold or anything. I'm the one who's pregnant. This baby is completely my responsibility."

"The hell it is," he replied, immediately contradicting her. "It's only half your responsibility. The other half is mine."

She didn't realize how much she'd been stressing over that until she felt the relief ease through her. She had steeled herself to hear Zane renounce all obligation to their child. Not that she would have accepted that—she would have at least filed for some kind of financial support. But to hear him so readily accept half the burden of everything that was to come was more than a little heartening.

But then, why was she surprised? This was a man who, when he was still almost a kid himself, had taken on the responsibility of raising four boys half his age. And he'd clearly done so with great success. She'd seen for herself what a good guy Zane was, even if she'd only spent a matter of hours with him. Of course he was a good guy. She wouldn't have fallen for him so quickly that night—or spent the night with him—if he hadn't been. Even so, he was adjusting to the news of his impending fatherhood awfully quickly...

He gave her one last hug then, with clear reluctance, released her and settled his hands on his hips. But he didn't move away. And he didn't stop beaming.

"Look, Sabrina, I realize that in spite of the fact that we somehow managed to create life together, you and

I really don't know each other that well. I understand why you might think I'd be put off by finding out you're pregnant, out of the blue, especially when we took precautions to avoid that."

"We're three-percenters," she said. "That's what the doctor told me. That condoms used correctly still fail three percent of the time."

"Yeah, well, I'd rather be a one-percenter," he said with a grin, "but I still don't mind being this particular statistic."

Sabrina didn't mind that, either, now that she was more used to the idea. Still, it was good to know she and Zane were of one mind on the matter.

He shrugged. "Truth is, I've pretty much been a father for the last ten years. And as scary as the thought of raising my brothers was in the beginning, over time, I got into the rhythm of it, even if it meant spending every second of my free time ferrying them around to football practice and clarinet lessons…gay-straight alliance meetings, chess club, drama club, film club…"

Here, his face lit up with another one of those heart-stopping, brilliant smiles, the kind she'd seen from him so often that night they spent together—as if he just couldn't believe how much he was loving the moment he was in. Something inside Sabrina went warm and gooey seeing it, the same way it had that night. And, as also had been the case that night, she wanted nothing more than to lean in and kiss him.

Had to be the pregnancy hormones, she told herself. She'd replayed that night in her mind a million times since it happened, and she'd come to the conclusion months ago that it had just been one of those strange nights where the stars aligned in a way to make both of them feel extraordinary and respond to the events—and each other—in ways they never would normally. And whatever that phenomenon was would never happen again. She'd come to that conclusion months ago, too.

"Now that the boys are all off to college," he continued, "I'm pretty much going through the whole empty nest thing people go through when they're suddenly alone after raising a family. But where those folks are in their fifties and sixties and looking toward a retirement where they can do all the fun stuff together that they've put off doing to raise a family, I won't be retiring for decades." He sighed. "And to be honest, a life that doesn't involve raising those boys doesn't feel like much of a life to me."

She tried to sound encouraging when she said, "I would think you'd be looking forward to some peace and quiet."

He shook his head. "I'm a family man, Sabrina, plain and simple. I realized that a long time ago. But my family's all out there embarking on their own lives now, and I've had no idea how I'm going to fill in all those gaps. Now that I know I'm about to become a real father..."

That beaming smile returned. Sabrina did her best not to swoon.

"Well, now. I suddenly have something to look forward to again. And I get to be the father to a baby! I missed out on all that with my brothers. By the time my oldest, Wyatt, was born, I was twelve and didn't want any part of babies. I wouldn't even babysit when my parents asked. I missed out on all the boys' firsts. First words, first steps, first solid food."

My oldest, Wyatt, Sabrina repeated to herself. She knew Zane had meant his oldest brother. But the way he talked, he sounded as if he were speaking of his oldest child. Though she supposed, in a way, he was. For all intents and purposes, for much of his siblings' lives, he'd been their father.

"After I became the boys' guardian," he continued, "that was the first time I really got to know any of them. And I found myself wishing I'd been around more for their early years. This time, for our baby, I'll be there from the beginning."

Our baby. Up until now, Sabrina hadn't been thinking about the life growing inside her in those terms. Mostly because she truly hadn't thought Zane would be all that enthusiastic about taking on the responsibility. Now that she realized he was already thinking in terms of *our baby...*

Well, actually, now that she thought about it, that was kind of scary. Just how much input did he want to have in this child's life? She'd been thinking she would be the primary decision maker for...oh, everything. From naming the child to picking out preschools to touring colleges when the time came. But Zane was right—he was equally responsible for her baby. *Their baby*, she hastily corrected herself. She just wasn't sure she wanted him to be. Her life really was going to be connected to his, for at least the next eighteen years. This man she barely knew would be invading the life of her and her child for the foreseeable future. And that...

Yeah. That was kind of scary.

It didn't help that he continued. "I didn't know what I was going to do with myself now that the boys are all off on their own. I haven't even had much interest in going on this trip, if you want the truth. But I didn't want to let my brothers down. They all worked so hard and invested so much. I'm sure I can at least get some of their money back, though."

"Wait, y-you're not going to take your trip of a life-time?" she stammered. "The one you had to postpone for ten years? The one you were so looking forward to?"

"Yeah, that trip. It's not as appealing now as it was when I was a kid. The closer it's gotten to time to leave, the less I've wanted to go. It just doesn't feel right, leaving the country for a whole year when the boys are still in college. I've kept thinking what if something happens and they need me? I could be on the other side of the planet. This trip…" He shrugged. "It just isn't as important to me as it was ten years ago. And it's certainly not once in a lifetime, like I thought it was then. I only thought that because I was young and figured I needed to do it before I got too old. But back then, 'too old' was, like, thirty."

He chuckled. But his levity didn't spill over onto Sabrina. She really was just beginning to realize how much impact Zane's impending fatherhood was going to have on her motherhood. She'd been working under the impression that he would stay in the periphery while she raised her child. But it was *their* child. She was going to have to include him in at least a few things. More than a few, if his reaction was any indication.

Then again, just how much thought had she actually put into this? It hadn't even been two full days since she found out she was going to be a mother. Even so, considering the circumstances, why wouldn't she think she would be the primary caregiver?

Very cautiously, she said, "Zane, just how involved are you planning to be in this baby's life?"

She might as well have just asked him if he wanted to drink hemlock, so stunned did he appear to be.

"What are you talking about?" he said. "We're going to co-parent, aren't we?"

He wanted to *co-parent*? she repeated incredulously to herself. Like split everything fifty-fifty? Which meant she would only see her child half of its life?

"Are we?" she asked with no small trepidation.

He looked even more confused. "Yeah… I mean, we're both the baby's parents. I want to be there for everything."

That didn't sound like *co-parenting* to Sabrina. That sounded like *parenting*. Parenting with a virtual stranger, at that. Which didn't seem like a good idea.

Wow, this conversation had gone right off the rails. Or maybe it had never even been on the rails. 'Cause it for sure wasn't going the way she'd planned.

"I wasn't exactly considering co-parenting this baby with you," she said honestly.

His dark brows knitted downward. "What exactly were you considering?"

She shook her head. "I'm not sure," she admitted. "I just came over today to let you know I was pregnant and that you're the father. I didn't expect…"

"What?" he said, his voice edged with challenge.

"I didn't expect you to want to be involved. Not to the point of actual parenting."

"Well, you were wrong," he said bluntly. "Why wouldn't I want to be involved in parenting my own child?"

"Because you just got your life back after raising four boys you'd never planned to raise," she reminded him. "And because—" She stopped herself before saying the last, because it sounded insulting even to her ears.

"Because what?" Zane demanded.

"Because you're trying to pull a land grab on a piece of property I need myself, and that's going to make things between us a bit sticky."

She waited for him to start fuming, to say something that would only ignite further the legal dispute that was simmering between them.

"I thought I was dealing with someone else until you told me you changed your name," he said. "And then you told me about the baby, and everything else in my head went south."

"Yeah, well, now you remember," she pointed out. "And now you understand it's going to be a thing between us."

He thought about that for a minute, then, said, "That's just business, Sabrina. It has nothing to do with us. Or our child."

"Oh, excuse me, but it has everything to do with us! And, by extension, our child."

He nodded, but the gesture was edged with something antagonistic. "Well, at least you're agreeing that it's *our* child. Like I said, the land thing is just business."

She'd been kind of hoping that once he realized she was the one he was trying to swindle, he would back off from his claim to the land. Obviously not. She knew all about *just business*. She was Casper Windham's daughter after all. Whenever her father had had to miss one of his children's major events—which had been often—it had been because of *just business*. Those nights when she'd come home from school excited to tell him about something that had happened and his chair had been empty at the dinner table because he had to work late had been just business. As had been those holidays when he was likewise absent from what should have been a fun event with the whole family. *Sabrina, you have to understand. It's just business.*

Maybe co-parenting with Zane wouldn't be such a big deal after all, she thought bitterly. Because if he was as *just business* as her father had been, she wouldn't be seeing much of him. And neither would their child.

What he said next only cemented that. "And you know what? There's no reason we can't approach co-parenting the same way. Like a business. You and I are both good at that. We'll just develop a successful model for co-parenting and follow it."

His comment about her being good at business, too, made her wince, mostly because she couldn't disagree with him. In a lot of ways, she was her father's daughter. She'd gone into business instead of pursuing her love of textile art because she'd sought his approval and known it would please him. How was she so sure she could put her child first when Casper had never been able to do that? Maybe she had a lot more to think about than she realized before she and Zane could come to any kind of consensus.

"I have to go," she said suddenly. "I just remembered someplace I'm supposed to be."

He looked more surprised by the statement than she had been to utter it. "But—"

"Really, Zane, I have to leave. We'll talk more later, 'kay?"

And then, without awaiting a reply, she spun on her heel and fled. She threw a quick thank-you to his housekeeper as she flew by, then raced out the door and sprinted to her car. From her rearview mirror, she saw Zane coming down the front steps, gesturing for her to come back. Sabrina didn't care. She wasn't going back. Not until she thought a lot more about his position in the life of her child—*their* child, she amended reluctantly. Bottom line? She needed to figure out how she felt about his presence in their child's life.

And, more to the point, how she felt about his presence in hers.

Sabrina had no idea where she was going after turning out of the long drive leading to Zane's house. At some point, she realized she was headed toward Chatelaine proper, so she just kept going in that direction. She hadn't eaten anything since that morning, and it was after lunch now. She might only be twelve-going-on-thirteen-weeks pregnant, but she was ravenous. The little person inside her must have some appetite. And as much as she was craving a cup of coffee—already she was having headaches from caffeine withdrawal after her decision to give it up for the duration of her pregnancy—a cup of herbal tea might be good for calming her frayed nerves.

As she approached the Daily Grind, she saw her sister Dahlia's car in the lot and immediately turned into it, too, to park a few spaces down. The bell over the coffee shop door rang cheerfully as she entered, and she quickly scanned the room for a familiar face. There was Sylvie, the wise-cracking waitress who had always been able to make Sabrina smile when she came in for her weekly macchiato. And, of course, there was Beau Weatherly, who all the Fortunes had learned pretty quick was Chatelaine's equivalent to Yoda or Dumbledore. Word around town said the sixtysomething retired ranch investor had an answer for just about any question a person could ask and insight into just about anything a person could need guidance on. He even had a sign on his table next to his iced coffee and scone that read Free Life Advice. Sabrina would have run to him right now for just that if he hadn't had a line waiting.

Finally, her gaze fell on not just Dahlia, but her sister Jade, too. They were seated at a wide round table in the back with three other women. She recognized two of them as two-thirds of the Perry triplets, Tabitha and Lily, whom she'd met shortly after her arrival in Chatelaine. Thanks to the third woman's resemblance to the other two Sabrina was going to go out on a limb and guess she was the third sister. Haley, she recalled. She knew all three women were involved with some of her newly acquired Fortune cousins, but she wasn't clear exactly who was married or engaged to whom—or if there even were marriages and engagements. Sabrina's newly discovered family was nothing if not large and prolific. Dahlia had formed a friendship with all three triplets, but her twin had always made friends more easily than Sabrina had. Jade looked pretty chummy with the sisters as well, though, so maybe it was time Sabrina stepped up and made their acquaintance, too.

As she made her way over to the table, Jade looked up and smiled, then waved hello and gestured her over. The other women all turned their attention to Sabrina as well, each smiling warmly in welcome.

"There's the little mama," Dahlia said as Sabrina moved to sit in an empty chair beside her.

When Sabrina snapped her head up to glare at her sister, Dahlia's smile faltered a little. "Just how many people have you told?" she asked her sister.

"Oops," Dahlia said, her smile turning sheepish. "But you never said not to tell anyone," she added.

True enough. And Sabrina knew her twin had fallen more easily into small-town life than she had herself, a big part of which was sharing any little bit of news one might have come across. Even so, she wasn't sure how ready she was to broadcast her condition. She'd told her siblings and her mother—and don't think Wendy wasn't delighted by the prospect of becoming a grammy—but since Sabrina didn't know many other people in Chatelaine except for Zane, she hadn't given much thought to telling anyone.

Not that it wouldn't become obvious before long. It might just be her imagination, but when she was showering that morning, she'd studied her belly and thought it already looked a little more rounded than usual. Still, she'd at least like to be comfortable with the knowledge herself before telling other people about it.

"Don't worry," Lily said. "Nothing stays secret in Chatelaine for long. We all would've known soon, anyway."

Sabrina didn't doubt it. Especially after the way Zane had just reacted. He was probably on his phone right now, texting the news to everyone he knew.

"At least she didn't tell them who the father is," Jade said in their sister's defense.

Tabitha's phone pinged on the table near her coffee cup, and she picked it up, reading the text that had appeared on the screen. "Zane Baston," she said matter-of-factly.

Sabrina's mouth dropped open in shock. "How do you know?"

"I just got a text from Lupe Cruz, who cuts my hair. Her husband's sister is a cattle hand on Night Heron Ranch."

Damn. Zane really was telling everyone he could think of.

The other triplets' phones pinged in quick succession, and each looked at their respective screens.

"Yep," Haley said. "Just heard from Blanche, my neighbor. Her brother, Evan, used to coach intramural flag football with Zane when his boys were in middle school with Zane's brothers."

"Mine is from Erin Margolis," Lily said. "She's married to Petey Margolis, whose mother was one of Zane's mother's closest friends when she was alive."

Unbelievable, Sabrina thought. The Chatelaine telegraph must be working overtime today.

All three women quickly texted responses—probably words to the effect of *We already know, what took YOU so long?*—then set their phones back on the table and looked at Sabrina.

"Zane's pretty dreamy," Haley said. "Great genes. You could do worse for your baby daddy."

"And he's such a nice guy," Lily added. "He's done so great with his brothers."

"Yeah, he'll be an awesome dad," Tabitha stated. "How did you two meet, anyway? You've only been in town a month."

Well, at least Dahlia had left out the part about it being a one-night stand. Not that there was anything wrong with one-night stands. Not unless you'd always been The Cautious One.

Before Sabrina could formulate an answer to that question, the bell over the coffee shop door rang again. Automatically, she turned to look at the new customer and saw a tall, handsome man with sandy blond hair searching the room in much the way she had upon entering, as if he were looking for someone specific. He had a slender manila envelope tucked under one arm and a hopeful expression on his face. When his gaze lit on their table, that expression turned even more buoyant, and he took a step in their direction, letting the door close behind him. But he hesitated after a couple more steps, as if uncertain about what his reception would be, before continuing to make his way across the shop.

When Dahlia saw Sabrina's gaze fixed on something behind her, she turned in her seat to see what she was looking at. Immediately, her jaw dropped, and she poked Sabrina in the side as she always had when they were kids and she needed to get her attention *fast*.

"Oh, my God," she whispered urgently. "It's *him*."

"Him who?" Sabrina whispered back. Dahlia really did seem to know everyone in Chatelaine already.

Her twin leaned in closer and lowered her voice even more. She threw a quick glance at the triplets, who were all still talking about Zane being such an amazing family man that they had yet to notice whoever this was coming toward them. "Heath Blackwood," Dahlia told her. "Rawlston and I met him right after he arrived in town. He was literally still pulling his suitcase behind himself. He was looking for the triplets. He's pretty sure he's their long-lost brother. And he just might be. The triplets have always suspected they're actually quadruplets. He told Rawlston and me that he'd discovered all kinds of genealogical info online that linked the four of them. He made us promise not to say anything to anybody, in case he's wrong—"

Oh, sure, Sabrina thought, Dahlia could keep *that* a secret for a total stranger.

"—but Haley and Tabitha and Lily never mentioned meeting him, so I guess their paths just haven't crossed yet."

Heath Blackwood came to a stop at their table, finally grabbing all the women's attention. Especially Jade's,

Sabrina couldn't help noticing. Her older sister actually kind of lit up at his arrival, even though Jade had never really been the lighting-up kind. He lifted the hand not holding the envelope to give his Stetson a polite tip. Then, as if just remembering his manners not to wear a hat indoors, he took it off completely.

"Excuse me, ladies, I don't mean to interrupt y'all's conversation, but I'm looking for—"

His gaze moved from the triplets to Dahlia, and he smiled when he recognized her.

"Well, hello there, Dahlia. It's good to see you again."

"You, too, Mr. Blackwood. I hope you've been enjoying your stay in Chatelaine." Before he could reply, Dahlia opened her hand toward the three women on the other side of the table. "May I introduce you to the Perry triplets?" She pointed at them each in turn as she said, "Lily, Tabitha, Haley, I'd like you to meet Heath Blackwood."

All three of the women smiled and greeted him warmly, but they also threw Dahlia a variety of curious looks.

Until Heath said, "Ladies, it's nice to meet you." He held up the manila envelope and added, "I believe the four of us are related. According to the information I have in here—" he gave the envelope a little shake "—I'm your brother."

Now the triplets' mouths dropped open in astonishment. Then, one after the other, they gasped. And then shot each other looks. And then smiled with delight.

Before they could say anything, though, Heath began speaking again. "I'm sorry it's taken me so long to talk to y'all. I just wasn't sure if it was the right thing to do. My family past is a bit murky." He nodded toward the manila envelope again. "But I've always been curious and finally checked one of those genealogy sites online and spit in the tube and sent it off. A few weeks ago, I got the results. They linked me to three women—each one of you—and said you were my sisters."

There was more gaping from the triplets. More gasps. More smiles.

"Oh, my God," Haley said. "We all took those tests, too, because we were hoping you might turn up! And you did!"

"It's true then?" Tabitha said. "The nice old lady from the GreatStore was right about there being four babies? We really are quadruplets instead of triplets?"

"But how did we get separated from our long-lost brother?" Lily asked.

"And how come we were never able to find a registry of your birth along with our own?" Tabitha added.

Heath looked more than a little confused by his sisters' reactions. He opened his mouth to say something, but they continued to speak, cutting him off, going on about the doctor who delivered them insisting there were only three babies, but Doris at the GreatStore insisting there were four she cared for after their parents' deaths when they were babies, one of whom was a boy.

"Ladies, hold up," Heath finally interjected. "I'm not a quadruplet. I'm not even your full brother. I'm your half brother. We have the same father. And I'm only older by two months."

Now the sisters were the ones to look confused.

"So that means our father had an affair?" Lily asked in clear shock.

"That doesn't make any sense," Haley added. "We always heard our parents were completely devoted to each other. Just what was going on thirty years ago?"

"I don't know," Heath admitted. "But I've already made up my mind that I'm moving here to Chatelaine to get to know what's left of my family. Maybe between the four of us, we can figure out the mystery. Starting with this…"

The sisters smiled in unison.

"We have a lot to talk about," Lily told him.

The other triplets nodded their agreement. Heath looked relieved.

"I was hoping you'd say that," he replied.

"Dinner at my place tonight," Haley said. "All of us together the way family should be. Just let us get the check, and we're outta here."

"Don't worry about it," Dahlia told them. "This one's on me."

"Me, too," Sabrina volunteered.

"But you didn't even have anything," Lily objected.

Sabrina smiled, their excitement and good cheer infectious. "Consider it a family-warming gift," she told them.

Dahlia nodded. "Yeah. Like a housewarming gift, only for a new family instead of a new home."

All four of the siblings grinned at that.

"New family," Tabitha echoed. "I like the sound of that."

"Me, too," Heath agreed.

Instinctively, Sabrina opened her hand lightly over the new life growing in her belly. *New family*, she repeated to herself. She liked the sound of it, too. She just hoped her own new family turned out to be as happy as the triplets-plus-one were promising to be.

She and her own sisters watched the newfound family make its way to the exit.

"How wild," Jade said. "It's like something from a soap opera. I'm amazed they were able to find each other."

"But they're together now," Sabrina said. "That's what's important. Family should always be together. In good times and in bad."

She told herself she wasn't being hypocritical when she said it. Just because she and Zane had produced a baby didn't make them family. Family was a lot more than genes and DNA. Biological parents was what she and Zane were. Nothing more. He had his family, she had hers, and their baby would be a part of both. Not a bad deal, really, having two families.

She just hoped the baby growing inside her felt that way, too.

Zane's brothers had all been out yesterday afternoon when Sabrina stopped by, making their final rounds about Chatelaine to tell their friends goodbye before heading off for their fall semesters. But he'd known they would all be home for dinner at the house tonight, so he'd saved the news of his impending fatherhood for that. He waited until they'd all finished the last of Astrid's famous lingonberry-cardamom cake—the boys' unanimous favorite, saved only for special occasions like this—to spring the news on them. As they passed their crumb-laden plates down to their youngest brother, Cody, who was assigned to kitchen duty this week, Zane told them to wait before leaving the table, because he had something to tell them.

They all gazed at him curiously, if not a little anxiously. The last time he'd told them he had news for them all at this table, it had been to reveal how he'd broken up with a girlfriend they'd all come to like a lot. Before that, it had been to tell them about the death of their golden retriever, Noodles. And the time before that, it had been their parents' deaths. Safe to say there hadn't been many happy announcements made at dinner in the Baston family.

Well, that was about to change. From now on, Zane vowed, there would be nothing but good news to pass along to his brothers.

"What happened now?" Wyatt asked. He looked too grave and earnest for his twenty-one years, his blue eyes intent behind his tortoiseshell glasses, his overly long auburn hair pushed back from his forehead.

"It's nothing bad," Zane hurried to assure them all. "Just something important y'all need to know about."

The twins, Shane and Levi, were nineteen years old and the closest in resemblance to Zane with their green eyes and dark hair. Even though they still looked a lot different from each other in every other aspect, they released an identical sigh of relief.

"So you're not going to tell us Gumbo had to go live on a farm in west Texas?" Levi asked.

Gumbo was the Australian shepherd they'd adopted after losing Noodles. He'd tried to tell them that classic fib about their late pet simply moving to another part of the state, but when you lived on a three-thousand-acre ranch, it was hard to convince a bunch of kids that their beloved dog was happier with more space to run around in.

"Gumbo is fine," Zane told them. "And so are Dumpling and Cornbread," he quickly added, verifying he had seen the semiferal cats who kept the barn free of vermin just that afternoon.

Though why the boys had always been so fixed on food names for their various pets, Zane would never know. If given the opportunity to name the baby he was about to tell them about, the poor kid would probably end up being Biscuit or Pork Chop.

"Then what's up?" Cody, the youngest at eighteen and the fairest of them all with his sandy hair and hazel eyes, asked.

As much as Zane had practiced in his head all afternoon how he wanted to tell the boys his news, he was still at a loss. He'd always prided himself on setting a good example for his brothers when it came to things like drinking and smoking and partying. The first he hadn't done much of in the first place, the second he'd never done at all and the third he'd curbed significantly after becoming their guardian. The girlfriend he'd broken up with three years ago had almost become his fiancée, which was the only reason the boys had met her in the first place. She'd been the only woman who hadn't taken off the minute she found out about his responsibility to four orphaned boys. He'd truly thought she was the one. Until he overheard her talking to a man he later found out was her husband about how much money they were going to make once she "married" him.

Yeah, that had been fun.

Anyway, how was he supposed to tell four impressionable young men, who were away from his influence altogether now that they were in college, that he'd had a one-night stand that resulted in an unplanned pregnancy? Even if he and Sabrina had taken precautions, that was pretty much a *Do as I say, not as I do* scenario, and Zane had always tried his best to avoid those.

He cleared his throat. "Okay, so it's kind of a good-news, bad-news situation," he began. "So I'll start with the bad."

"You said it wasn't bad," Shane reminded him.

Damn. Already caught in a lie. Those kids were too smart for their own good.

"Okay, it's not *that* bad," he amended. "But I'm going to have to postpone my trip around the world."

"What?" the boys cried in unison before they began barking out individual objections one after another.

Zane lifted a hand to quiet them. "I said postpone, not cancel," he reiterated. "I'll still go around the world someday. Just…not for a while yet."

His brothers began to protest again, so Zane lifted his other hand to quiet them. "There's a good reason for it," he promised.

"It better be good," Wyatt told him. "You've been looking forward to this since before Mom and Dad died."

"I know," he said. "And y'all sacrificed a lot personally for me, and I can't thank you enough for that. But here's the thing, guys." Zane smiled, letting his absolute happiness about what he was to tell them shine through. "I found out yesterday that I'm going to be a father. And you're all going to be uncles."

For a moment, none of the boys said a word. Then, as one, they whooped and hollered almost as much as Zane had when Sabrina told him the news.

"What are you talkin' about?" Shane said with a laugh.

"How did this happen?" Wyatt added, chuckling.

"Who's the mother?" Levi wanted to know.

"When's the baby gonna be here?" Cody demanded.

Oh, boy, Zane thought. He truly hadn't thought about all the questions he was going to have to answer. Instead of going in order, he went with easiest first.

"What I'm talking about is a new member of our family. By the time you guys come home for spring break next year, Baby Baston will be here. And how it happened is exactly the way all of us learned about in sixth grade health class."

The boys were still looking at him expectantly. Zane hoped if he stopped here, they'd forget about the *who*.

"And the baby mama?" Wyatt asked.

Zane sighed. He should've known better.

"She's a very nice lady I met at a fundraiser a while back," he told them. "She and I hit it off, one thing led to another and…" He scrunched up his shoulders and let them drop. "Neither one of us planned for this to happen, obviously. And we used protection," he added pointedly. "We were just part of that small percentage where it fails. Which should be a lesson to all y'all," he added firmly.

But all the boys did was smile goofily at him.

"Anyway, it did happen," Zane continued, "and now we're going to try to make the best of it. That's why I have to postpone the trip. So I can be here to help with anything she needs during the pregnancy and birth and whatever comes after that."

"What's her name?" Levi asked.

"Sabrina," he answered simply. His brothers waited for a last name, but before they could push it, he hurried on. "You don't know her. She was living in Dallas when we met."

Too late, he realized his mistake in saying even that much.

"You haven't been to Dallas in years," Cody said. "And you've dated a few women since then. Just how long have you known your baby mama?"

Damn. Busted again.

"All right, fine. She and I had a little one-night fling when she was visiting Chatelaine a few months ago. We took precautions," he told them again. "Which should be a lesson to all of you," he added again. "Don't mess around." There. Teachable moment taught.

All four boys only laughed. "Oh, no you don't," Wyatt said. "You're not going to turn this around on us. You're gonna be a daddy!"

His brothers went back to their whooping and hollering and calling each other Uncle Whatever. Then they started throwing out names, starting with characters from their favorite games—Geralt! Shepherd! Tom Nook!—to their favorite books—Septimus! Montmorency! Percy!

Then Cody said, "Wait, what if it's a girl?"

His brothers—and Zane, for that matter—looked at him as if he'd grown a third eye.

"It's not going to be a girl," Wyatt told him with much conviction. "Bastons are never girls. Dad was an only child, but Grampa had brothers. Great-grampa had brothers." He looked at Zane. "Has there ever been a girl Baston in this family that didn't marry into it?"

"Not that I ever heard," Zane told them.

Which was just as well, since having raised four boys, Zane wasn't sure he would have the first clue how to raise a baby girl.

After a lot more back and forth debate over what to name the kid—whether it ended up being a boy *or* a girl—all his brothers did finally agree on one thing: that whatever bedroom was assigned to the baby here at the house, that room would *not* be any of theirs. Which was fine with Zane. His parents' room had been vacant since their deaths. It hadn't even been used for a guest room. But his folks would definitely be smiling down from Heaven when they saw their first grandbaby occupying that room after them.

"Better get yourself used to unicorns and fairies," Wyatt said for good measure, clearly not convinced that the baby being a girl was out of the question.

"Very funny," Zane retorted. "I'm just glad we still have some of y'all's hand-me-downs around here somewhere. Those cowboy pajamas and Tonka trucks are going to come in handy pretty quick."

"Well, we're sorry you're going to have to put off the trip," Cody said, "but at least it's for a good reason."

"The best," Zane agreed. "And I made some calls today, and I was able to get ninety-nine percent of the trip refunded, either in cash or travel vouchers. So anytime I want to go in the future, I can. Who knows? Maybe Sabrina and I can take the trip together for a late honeymoon."

All four of his brothers' eyes nearly bugged out of their heads. Only when Zane saw their expressions did he realize he had spoken aloud a thought that he had vaguely entertained—and quickly discarded—after Sabrina's abrupt departure yesterday afternoon. A million thoughts had cartwheeled through his head as he considered every possible aspect of their situation, one of which had been a marriage of convenience for the sake of the child. Why not? Those kind of marriages had been around for millennia and were still a time-honored tradition in a lot of places. And, hell, people got hitched for worse reasons.

The idea had only hung around for a minute or two, though. Now that Sabrina lived here in Chatelaine, it wouldn't be that difficult for the two of them to co-parent their child from their respective homes. They could work out the logistics and arrangements with an attorney before the baby's arrival. Fifty-fifty time, he'd figured. A week at her place, a week at his. Or two weeks apiece. Even trading off every other month could be manageable, because they could still do stuff with their child in between times. They had plenty of time to work it out, he'd decided. Marriage didn't really have to be an option, even for the sake of convenience.

Did it?

"Wait, what? Honeymoon? You two are getting *married*?" Wyatt asked before Zane had a chance to explain any of that.

Cody, of course, had to take it one step further. "Big brother, are you in love with this Sabrina?"

Of course he wasn't in love with Sabrina. That was ridiculous. He barely knew her. Besides, he'd sworn off love a long time ago. Romantic love didn't exist as far as he was concerned. At least not for him. He'd seen it faked too many times to believe it was real.

"My feelings for Sabrina are...complicated," he finally told his brothers. "There. That's a word you young people use, right? And no, I'm not saying Sabrina and I will be getting married. I'm not saying anything until she and I get to talk about this some more."

"Then why do you sound *a lot* like you wanna marry her?" Levi asked.

"Yeah," Shane agreed. "You sure seemed confident when you said the trip could be your honeymoon."

"That was just—" Zane expelled a restless sound. Dammit, he hated it when his brothers got all know-it-all on him. And not just because, too often, they were right. "I was just weighing all my options. And I really don't think that's one of them." He hurried to hammer that home when he saw Cody about to object, too. Once that kid got an idea about something, he never let it go.

"Look," he told his brothers, "Sabrina and I still have

a lot to talk about where the baby is concerned. But I wanted y'all to hear about it from me first. Word's already spreading like wildfire around town."

Which, in hindsight, he should have known would happen even though he'd only told two people—his foreman, Mateo, and Millie Santiago, Chatelaine's sole travel agent. But he'd sworn both to secrecy. Which, okay, had been a stupid thing to ask for in a small town like Chatelaine.

Wow. Hindsight really was twenty-twenty.

"But Sabrina and I will work it all out," he assured his brothers.

And they would, he assured himself, too. Just as soon as they figured out how the hell to do that.

Chapter Four

It was just past nine when Sabrina heard a knock at her front door. She was freshly showered and wearing her pajamas—pale lilac cotton this time with a matching T-shirt—and had just brewed a cup of chamomile tea. To say she was surprised was an understatement. The only people she'd had at her house since moving in were members of her family. Certainly everyone in Chatelaine knew the Fortunes had bought the old Madison property, but considering how many houses were on the place, there was little chance anyone would know which of the log homes belonged to which Fortune sibling short of driving past each one looking for their respective cars.

She checked the app for her doorbell camera before going to answer and was even more surprised when she saw Zane standing under the porch light, his Stetson in one hand and what looked like a small box in the other. Looked like the driving by to identify the cars thing had occurred to him, too. She knew she should have parked in the garage.

The two of them hadn't exactly ended things on great terms earlier in the week, what with her fleeing his house without even saying goodbye—the second time she'd done that, she couldn't help thinking. She'd kind of hoped she could avoid him for a bit longer before having to see him again.

Apparently that wish hadn't been granted.

With a resigned sigh, she left her tea on the kitchen counter, tucked a few errant strands of hair into the messy bun she'd slung atop her head before her shower and made her way to the door. By the time she turned the knob and opened it, Zane was halfway down the front steps, having evidently given up on her answering. He spun around at the click of the dead bolt, however, and smiled at her with more than a little relief.

"Hey," he said softly by way of a greeting.

"Hello," she replied just as quietly.

"I'm sorry to stop by so late," he told her. "But I haven't gotten a wink of sleep the last couple nights, and tonight wasn't going to be any different. I don't think I'll be sleeping again until the two of us get a few things settled."

She nodded. "Yeah, I get that. My brain has been pretty noisy the last few days, too." She opened the door wider. "Come on in. It's not that late."

His clear relief turned to gratitude as he climbed the steps again. But he hesitated a moment at the threshold, as if he still wasn't sure of his welcome. So Sabrina pushed the door open more and took a few steps backward, giving him a wide berth.

Not quite wide enough, though, not to notice how good he smelled, a mix of leather and sandalwood. He'd showered, too, before coming over. His hair was even still a little damp, she noted, curling a little at his nape.

It was all she could do not to reach out and run her fingers over it to flatten it out. He'd obviously changed into fresh clothes, too, dark jeans and western-style shirt the color of a pine forest.

He truly was one of the most handsome men she had ever seen. Haley Perry was right. She could have done a lot worse, gene-pool-wise, for her baby's father.

"I was just fixing some tea," she said as she closed the door behind him. "Would you like some? Or a cup of coffee?"

He was shaking his head before she even finished the question. "Thanks, I'm good." He extended the box toward her. "But I brought you some cookies Astrid made this afternoon. She calls them havreflarns."

Sabrina chuckled at the name. It was a funny-sounding dessert coming from a woman who looked like she could tear a kraken in half with her bare hands.

She opened the box long enough to see what looked like a dozen very thin oatmeal cookies. And, unable to resist, she lifted one out to sample it, too. Definitely oatmeal cookies, but super crispy oatmeal cookies. She was about to put the lid back on the box, but grabbed one more cookie to join what was left of the first in her other hand before doing so. When she looked up at Zane, he was grinning.

"Yeah, they're a fave around our house."

"I'm eating for two," she reminded him.

His grin broadened. "Did I say anything?"

No, he didn't. And she had to admit she kinda loved him for that.

"Tell Astrid I said thank you," she said.

"I will."

She nodded toward the living room. "Come on in."

Sabrina had started a fire in the big stone fireplace before making her tea, and it had caught nicely by the time they entered. The tawny log walls glowed like satin in the firelight, and shadows danced merrily on the vaulted ceiling. As he followed her inside, she was aware that the only other light in the room was the buttery glow from a single torchère in the corner, making the space look even cozier in spite of its sparse furnishings. She crossed the wide, Navajo-print rug to take a seat on a sofa the color of cream, pushing herself into a far corner to give Zane plenty of room in case he wanted to sit there, too.

Instead, he folded himself into the matching chair beside it. Still close, but far enough way that she knew he was deliberately giving her some space. She kind of loved him for that, too. She nibbled her first cookie nervously before realizing her appetite had disappeared, so she placed both on top of the box she'd laid on the coffee table. Zane set his Stetson on the table, too, then leaned back in the chair and looked at Sabrina intently.

"So," he said. But he didn't elaborate.

"So," she echoed.

For a moment, the room descended into silence broken only by the crackle of the fire, Sabrina and Zane gazing at each other as if neither had the first clue what they were doing there.

Finally, Zane said, "We're going to have a baby."

Sabrina nodded. "Yes, we are."

"That, um, that's kind of a big deal."

"It is."

"I'm sorry if I said something the other day that—" he sighed heavily "—that didn't sit right with you. You took me by surprise when you left in such a hurry. I guess I might have overreacted a little."

"No, it wasn't that," Sabrina told him. "I think I just hadn't put enough thought into it myself before breaking the news to you. I was thinking in terms of what *I* was going to do about the baby. Not what *we* were going to do. It truly hadn't occurred to me that you might want to be as deeply involved as I'm obviously going to be. And I don't want you to take that the wrong way," she said quickly. "It's not that I thought you'd be coldhearted and disinterested. It was that I just didn't consider you in the equation. I was too busy panicking for myself. That's why I took off."

He studied her in silence for a moment. "I guess I get that," he said. "I can't imagine what it must be like for a woman to realize she suddenly has someone else to think about for the rest of her life. And I know a lot of guys don't step up to the plate for that." He leaned forward in his seat. "But, Sabrina, I'm not one of those guys. I *want* to have to think about someone else for the rest of my life. Maybe I won't be growing this baby inside myself and pushing it out later, but I want to be just as involved as you are with everything else that I can be."

"And I get that," she told him. "But…it's complicated, Zane."

"It only seems complicated now because it's so new," he assured her. "And because you and I need to get to know each other better. I think if we talk through it, and we give it some time, we'll figure out it's not nearly as convoluted as it seems right now."

She knew what he said made sense. But what he said also meant the two of them needed to spend more time together. Which, yes, also was logical. But there was a part of Sabrina that kind of liked knowing so little about Zane. Not knowing him made it easier for her to mold him into whatever she wanted him to be. And what she wanted him to be was a man who would keep his distance. She'd spent the last ten years avoiding entanglements because she hadn't wanted to experience the grief and heartbreak that came with loving and losing someone again.

Not that she thought she would fall in love with Zane. She'd pretty much come to the conclusion that she would never fall in love again. Not a single man she'd dated since Preston's death had come close to being important to her. In fact, no one she'd dated had lasted more than a few months. Not because any of them had been off-putting in any way. On the contrary, it had taken a lot for a man to interest her enough to date him in the first place. But that was just the point. None of those infinitely likable, attractive men had done anything for her. Ergo, she just wasn't going to love anyone the way she'd loved her husband.

But even after seeing Zane only briefly the other day, knowing he was half-responsible for the life growing inside her, she was already coming to...have feelings for him. Just what those feelings were, though, she had no idea. And she didn't know where they were coming from, either. Was she drawn to him because he was Zane Baston, good guy? Or was it because he was Zane Baston, baby daddy? And who knew if those feelings—whatever they were—would last any longer than her pregnancy?

"That night of the fundraiser," he began again when she didn't respond, "you and I talked about a lot of things. The work you were doing for your nonprofit, my plans to expand Night Heron Ranch, the books and movies we loved when we were kids, where to find the best Tex-Mex in the state…"

Sabrina managed a chuckle for that. "I still say Austin."

"And I still say Amarillo."

"Agree to disagree," she said with a smile.

"If memory serves, we agreed to disagree about a lot of things that night. I still can't believe you don't like George Strait."

"I never said I didn't like him," she replied. "I just said I was more of a Miranda Lambert girl."

He shook his head hopelessly. "And you like the Astros more than the Rangers."

She shrugged. "One of my friends from college is married to an Astro," she explained.

He sighed melodramatically. "At least you like the Dallas Cowboys."

Sabrina wrinkled her nose a bit. "Actually, I only said that to make you happy after the Astros-Rangers thing. I'm really not much of a football fan at all."

He feigned shock. "Are you sure you were born in Texas?"

She laughed lightly. "Ask me about my chicken-fried steak addiction."

Zane's smile went supernova. Sabrina tried not to melt. "Well, alright then," he said. "Now we can talk about co-parenting this kid."

The way he was looking at her now was a lot like the way he looked at her that night at the fundraiser, when they first started to realize that something— something flirty and warm and appealing—was happening between them. If things kept going the way they did then, that something would soon turn into sensuous and hot and arousing. And although Sabrina didn't have a moon-drenched rose garden outside for them to dance to for stolen kisses, the golden firelit living room was becoming every bit as romantic, every bit as tempting. Zane was tempting in that moment, too. Because those thoughts of moonlight and kisses were starting to take over thoughts about…oh, everything else.

He seemed to realize the avenue her ruminations were wandering, because his smile suddenly fell, and his gaze turned smoky and hot, as if he were now thinking about the way that night had ended up, too. Without thinking, she pulled her legs up in front of herself, wrapping her arms tightly around her knees. Though whether she'd completed the gesture to keep Zane at bay or to keep herself from acting on her impulses, she honestly didn't know.

Pregnancy hormones, she tried to tell herself again. But something told her it was an entirely different set of hormones at play just then.

"I, um, I'm just not, ah, not sure where to begin," she stammered.

And she wasn't just talking about the baby now, she realized. Suddenly, it seemed like she and Zane should be making plans and rules for themselves, too.

She blew out an unsteady breath. "Every time I start thinking about the two of us trying to bring this child up together-but-not-together, my brain just freezes."

The word *freezes* had the desired effect on both of them. Zane's thoughts about the two of them seemed to cool along with her own when she brought up the topic of the baby again.

"What if we don't have the same vision for child-rearing?" she continued. "What if my idea of boundaries and rules is completely different from yours? And if they have to live one way at my place and a different way at yours, that's just going to confuse the poor kid." She grimaced. "That's no way to raise a well-adjusted little human."

"We have six months to work that out," he said. "And for the things we don't agree on, we'll just compromise and stick to whatever arrangement we come up with."

"It's not just that," she told him. "It's the whole splitting locations. Our child is going to be shuttling from one house to another for their entire childhood and adolescence. That's not a good way to establish a sense of permanence."

"Kids of divorce live that way all the time, Sabrina," Zane pointed out. "And they turn out just fine."

"But most kids of divorce have one primary parent and one primary residence that serves as an anchor of sorts. Our child, if we co-parent, won't have a primary at all. It will all be fifty-fifty. I worry they won't be able to bond well with either of us."

Zane looked at her for a moment in silence. Then he blew out a long, ponderous breath. "Okay, then, how would you feel about a marriage of convenience?"

Sabrina was sure she misheard. *"What?"* she asked.

"A marriage of convenience," he repeated. "You and I get married and live together and raise the child at Night Heron Ranch. You could have your own room," he added quickly when her disagreement with the suggestion must have shown on her face. "But we'd both be in one place for our child twenty-four-seven."

Putting aside, for the moment, the fact that the thought of marrying anyone, for any reason, was the most disagreeable thing she could imagine, she asked, "Why Night Heron Ranch? Why couldn't we live here?"

His eyebrows shot up to his hairline. "You mean you'd actually consider it?"

"Of course not!" she told him. "I'm just saying you're being awfully presumptuous to think we should live at your place, just because you're the man."

"It's not just because I'm the man. It's because I have a working ranch I need to be present every day to work on. You work at your ranch office. You can live anywhere in town."

"Oh, sure. Spoken like a self-entitled man who's had his way from the day he was born just because he's, you know, a man."

Instead of arguing with her, Zane bit back another smile. "Is this our first newlywed spat?" he asked.

"'Cause this feels like a newlywed spat to me. You're just trying to pick a fight to push the envelope and see what you can get away with in this marriage."

Sabrina did her best to look peeved. Then she smiled, too. "No, it's not a newlywed spat. For one thing, we're not newlyweds. Nor will we be," she added adamantly. "Because we're *not* getting married. Especially not for the sake of convenience."

Sabrina had sworn since losing her husband that she would only ever marry again for love. And since it had become clear over the last ten years that love wasn't going to happen for her again, neither was marriage.

Zane's relief that she had turned down his proposal was almost palpable. His gaze dropped to her lap, and, very softly, he said, "But we still need to figure out how we're both going to be present in this little buckaroo's life without joining ours."

As had been the case all week, every time Sabrina thought about the baby, she opened a hand protectively over her belly. "Yeah, we do," she said just as quietly.

"It'll be okay, Sabrina," he promised her. "If we don't approach this from a marriage-of-convenience stance, maybe we could go back to looking at it like a business arrangement. You and I are both savvy businesspeople. There's no reason why we can't run our family the same way we would a business."

There it was again. Him thinking they could raise a child the same way they could run a corporation. What was that old saying about women always marrying their fathers? Good thing Sabrina wasn't marrying Zane.

She spoke carefully as she said, "Okay, supposing

we do approach this co-parenting thing the same way we would if we were starting a new venture together."

He nodded once. "Alright. Let's think about that."

"First thing we need to start a business is a solid plan."

"Sounds good."

"We can bypass naming the company until the time comes, and we'll work on the mission statement as we go."

Zane nodded. "Both of those are pretty self-explanatory, anyway."

"Right. And we don't really have to go into products and services or a market analysis."

"Agreed."

"Financials?" she asked.

"I think we're both good there."

She pointed a finger knowingly. "Budget," she said. "We need to figure out a budget for monthly expenses."

"Since you're the accountant, I'll leave that to you."

"I'll work one out tomorrow."

"Okay, so what's left?" Zane asked. "'Cause this business isn't really sounding like much of a business to me at this point."

"Yeah, co-parenting doesn't really seem to lend itself to incorporation, does it? Though I guess we could use some aspects of a business model. Make up some spreadsheets for feeding times and flow charts for visitations. What do you think?"

He made a face at that. "When you put it like that, not much. Maybe my only parenting experience is with my brothers and never involved babies, but I can tell you one thing. You can't flow chart or spreadsheet any of it."

She sighed. Point made. "So then the business approach to co-parenting doesn't sound like a very good one, either."

They really did have a lot to muddle through. She just hoped it wasn't more than they could cover in six months. She expelled a restless sound but Zane smiled reassuringly.

"Look, Sabrina, I know neither of us planned this thing, but it is starting to feel kind of weirdly right, you know? Like it happened for a reason or something. I'm not much of a believer in fate, but I do feel like this baby will be a good thing. For both of us."

She smiled. "Once we figure it all out. Which I'm sure we'll do. Any day now."

Zane smiled back. "Next week's pretty open for me. How about you?"

"I have an appointment for an ultrasound on Wednesday," she told him. "I don't suppose there's any chance you'd like to come with me, is there?"

His smile went supernova. "You mean get to meet my kid in all his, uh, sound waves? Count me in!"

It was the first time either of them had used a specific pronoun to refer to the baby. "What makes you think it's a he?"

"It's gotta be," Zane told her with complete confidence. "There hasn't been a girl born in the Baston line for as many generations back as I can remember."

"There's a first time for everything," Sabrina reminded him.

"Not for this," Zane told her. "We're having a son, Sabrina. Mark my words. You can count on that as sure as you can count on bluebonnets in the spring."

Zane stood with his back turned in the sonogram room at Sabrina's doctor's office while she made herself comfortable on the padded table. He knew he probably looked ridiculous to the ultrasound technician—they'd already had to correct the receptionist and one nurse that they weren't a couple, just, you know, having a baby together. He listened while Sabrina patiently explained it to the tech, too. The tech who replied with yet another platitude about *Hey, that's cool, lots of people are doing that these days*, when, in fact, Zane couldn't think of a single other couple in Chatelaine—or anywhere else for that matter—who'd just woken up one morning and thought, *This is a good day to plan an unplanned pregnancy with someone I've only known a matter of hours*. Yeah, times had changed since previous generations, but they hadn't changed that much.

"You can turn around now," he heard Sabrina say.

When he did, he saw her lying with her shirt pushed up just under her breasts, a paper blanket covering her lower half and her torso completely exposed. Maybe he was only imagining things, but it looked to him like she was already showing a little bit. There was an elegant curve to her belly that hinted at the fact that there was something going on down there besides the digestion of the breakfast they'd shared together at the Cowgirl Café that morning. He found himself wondering how long it would be before they could feel the little guy moving around in there.

He took a step toward her, then hesitated. Just how close was he supposed to be for this thing?

"You won't be able to see anything from there," the tech told him. "Come on over."

She didn't have to tell him twice. He moved to stand immediately beside the table, his eyes darting from Sabrina's face to the black sonogram screen, then back to Sabrina's face again. Her expression was a mix of excitement and anxiety, the same things he was feeling himself.

"Deep breath," she told him, before taking one herself.

Zane did likewise, and, together, they released it. Yeah. That helped.

"Alrighty," the tech said as she fired up her equipment. "Let's see what we've got going on in there."

The badge she had clipped to her lanyard said her name was Patsy Barnard. She was old enough to be somebody's grandmother, but she had a bright stripe of rainbow colors streaking through her white hair from her forehead to the tip of the loose braid at her nape. Her reading glasses were as speckled as a bag of Skittles, and she was wearing hot pink lipstick paired with lime green fingernails. Zane figured they were in good hands with Patsy.

"Now, the gel is gonna be a little cold when it hits your tummy," she told Sabrina, "but it'll warm up fast."

"Thanks for the warning," Sabrina told her.

Even so, she squealed a bit at first contact. Zane chuckled, they shared one more smile, then both turned their heads to watch the screen. At first, it was just black with some gray blobs floating around. Patsy said she was going to check out not just the baby, but the placenta and Sabrina's uterus and fallopian tubes, to make sure everything looked the way it was supposed to. She told them that in addition to making sure the baby was indeed thirteen weeks at this point—which Sabrina and Zane could've told her the exact moment of conception—she would look for any sign of problems and even measure the baby to see how big it currently was.

"And there it is," she said.

All Zane saw was a bunch of gray squiggly lines with a few blotches of white moving around them. Thankfully, Patsy pointed to one of those blotches of white and said, "There's y'all's baby. Almost two and half inches. 'Bout the size of a peach."

"Peach," Sabrina repeated softly. "That's our baby, Peach, Zane."

He smiled. So they already had a nickname. It fit. He liked it. And it was a food name, so his brothers would love it, too. He felt Sabrina's hand weave itself with his, her fingers curling tight with his own. When he looked down from the screen, she was looking at him, her eyes damp with tears. But she said nothing more. Which he totally got. There were no words for what he was feeling, either.

Patsy was about to say something else, but stopped, her mouth still open. She moved the wand around on Sabrina's belly some more, then paused.

"Let's turn on the sound to see if we can hear a heartbeat," she said.

When she did, all Zane heard was some scratchy, bloopy sounds. But then, when he focused more intently, he heard it. The *lub-dub, lub-dub, lub-dub* of their baby's heartbeat.

"Wow, that's really fast," he said. "Is a baby's heartbeat supposed to be that fast?"

He and Sabrina both turned to look at Patsy. Who was now, he couldn't help noticing, grinning from ear to ear.

Immediately, however, she reined in her smile and cleared her throat. "Yanno," she said, "lemme just see if I can get Dr. Brewer in here now instead of after we're finished."

Before either of them could say another word, the tech was off of her stool and out the door, the ultrasound wand still sitting on Sabrina's midsection. Zane looked at Sabrina. Sabrina looked at Zane. An unmistakable frisson of fear arced between them.

"Why would she need the doctor?" Sabrina asked.

"And why in such a hurry, before we're even done with the ultrasound?" Zane replied. "I mean, she was smiling there for a minute, so surely there's nothing wrong, right?"

Sabrina nodded. But she didn't look anywhere near convinced. He wasn't convinced, either. Especially when several long minutes passed before Patsy and Dr. Brewer returned. The tech was still smiling, though, something that quelled Zane's fears a little. Dr. Brewer was looking noncommittal, but she didn't look worried, so there was at least that.

"Let's just have a look-see at this ultrasound, shall we?" the doctor said.

She looked to be in her fifties, with chin-length salt-and-pepper hair and no-nonsense black readers perched on the bridge of her nose. Her own lanyard, in addition to holding her ID, was decorated with assorted enamel pins of women's reproductive parts and a button that said, "May the forceps be with you," so it was hard for Zane to stay worried.

Sabrina, however, still sounded concerned when she asked, "Is everything okay?"

Neither of the other women replied right away. Instead, Dr. Brewer took a moment to study the screen and listen to the sound of what still sounded to Zane like a much-too-fast heartbeat.

"Is the heartbeat supposed to be that fast, Dr. Brewer?" he asked.

Dr. Brewer looked at Zane, then Sabrina. Then she smiled brightly. "It's not that the heartbeat is particularly fast," she said. "It's that you're hearing two of them."

Zane didn't understand. Did ultrasounds normally echo like that? Was the equipment malfunctioning? When he glanced down at Sabrina, she looked as confused as he was.

"Is this thing working right?" he asked, pointing at the ultrasound machine.

Dr. Brewer nodded. "Oh, yes," she told him. "It's working perfectly. And so are you, Sabrina," she added with a smile for her charge. "Everything looks and sounds exactly as it should in there. You are right at thirteen weeks along." She pointed to a white area on the sonogram screen. "This is your baby, who Patsy tells me you're calling Peach."

Sabrina nodded, but said nothing.

"But Peach isn't alone in there," Dr. Brewer said. She moved her hand to another white patch immediately to Peach's left. "This is your other baby."

When neither Sabrina nor Zane said anything in reply, Dr. Brewer grinned nearly as big as Patsy had. "You're having twins, Sabrina."

Sabrina's eyes went wide, and Zane's mouth dropped open.

Twins? he repeated incredulously to himself. That meant two, right? He remembered he had twin brothers. And that, yep, there were two of them. The word *twins* definitely referred to *two*. Sabrina was also one of two sets of twins in her own family. So there it was—three whole examples of how *twins* ran in both their families, and twins definitely meant *two*. For some reason, though, the implication of what Dr. Brewer just told them couldn't quite gel in his brain.

"Twins?" Sabrina asked.

"That's right," the doctor told her.

Even after hearing the word from Sabrina, Zane couldn't quite grasp the idea of two babies growing inside her. Two babies that were half her and half him. Two babies. Two *babies*. *Two* babies.

Oh, yeah, there it was. The realization of exactly what this meant. It stabbed him in the middle of his brain with all the force of two storks zooming out of the cabbage patch.

"Wow." Sabrina stared at the screen, her expression bordering on incoherent. "I thought...or maybe I just wondered... I mean I never suspected... Okay, yeah, I'm a twin... And my brother and sister are, you know..." She didn't finish the sentence, as if she were afraid to say the word again. "And Zane's brothers are...too, but I thought that the odds of having even more...was just... Holy cow!"

"Yes, indeed," Dr. Brewer said with another smile.

"Y'all want to know their sex?" Patsy asked. "Boys? Girls? One of each? 'Cause we can probably find that out, too, if you want."

Zane looked at Sabrina. Sabrina looked at Zane. As one, they smiled and said, "Yes."

Patsy took her seat on the stool again, picked up the sonogram wand from Sabrina's belly, then started maneuvering it around to get a better look. Sabrina's and Zane's attention, however, remained totally fixed on each other.

"Twins," Sabrina murmured again, pushing the word out of her mouth as if she were just learning it.

"Yeah," he said thickly. "How about that?"

Patsy interrupted by crying out, "It's two girls!"

"Congratulations to you both," Dr. Brewer told them. "I have two daughters myself. Daughters are wonderful."

Daughters? Zane repeated to himself. His brain couldn't process that word any better than it had *twins*.

The Baston line was about to welcome its first girls? He was going to have *daughters*? *Two* of them?

Wow. Gosh. Huh. How about that?

"Peach's sister is a bit smaller," Patsy told them, "but still perfectly within normal size. About as big as a plum."

"Peach and Plum," he heard Sabrina repeat with quiet wonder. "We're having a Peach and a Plum, Zane."

Peach and Plum, he repeated to himself. Sisters. Twin sisters. Two twin sisters.

"Zane?" he heard Sabrina say again. But his name seemed to be coming from the bottom of an ocean a million miles away. "Are you okay?"

He nodded but wasn't sure he trusted himself to be able to form any words that made sense.

"You don't look so good," she added.

"He'll be fine," Dr. Brewer said. "I've seen that look before. You just need to take him home and fix him a pot of strong coffee."

"Or pour him a stiff bourbon," Patsy added.

Or both, Zane thought. Yeah, both sounded good.

Vaguely, he heard Sabrina's doctor giving her instructions on how Sabrina should care for herself and the twins growing inside her. Then he heard Patsy say something about how she would print two sets of images from the sonogram of the twins for her and Zane to show around until they had the official newborn photos six months, or even less, from now. He obediently turned his back again when Sabrina asked him to so that she could get dressed, then back again when she told him she was ready. Well, that made one of them.

Then, somehow, the two of them made it out to the reception desk where Sabrina settled the insurance info and scheduled her next appointment, and out to the parking lot where Zane had parked his truck.

It registered on some level that he was sitting in the driver's seat and needed to start the engine and get them to wherever they were supposed to be going. Problem was, he didn't know where they were supposed to be going. In more ways than one.

"You want me to drive?" he heard Sabrina ask from the bottom of that faraway ocean again.

He shook his head. "Just give me a minute."

"Okay."

Twins. Girls. Zane was about to become the father of two daughters.

"Twins," he said aloud.

"Yes," Sabrina confirmed unnecessarily.

"Two girls."

"Yep. You okay with that?"

Zane gave himself a minute to think about how to answer that question. But he immediately realized he didn't need any time at all. He was okay. He was more than okay. He was about to become a father. A real life, honest-to-God father. Of not just one, but two kids. Girls. Which, yeah, came as a surprise, but was still…

Wow. The idea of having daughters was suddenly really, really cool. Maybe he hadn't expected it, but the idea of two little girls running around a house that had only known little boys until now seemed like it was going to be a lot of fun. Once he figured out how to handle two little girls.

"I'm more than okay," he told Sabrina, turning to her with a smile. "And how are you?"

She grinned back. "It's going to take some getting used to, but…I'm more than okay, too."

He shook his head once, to clear it of what little fuzziness remained. Then he turned the key in the ignition and started the truck.

"We should go somewhere to celebrate," he said. "Have a glass of champagne or something."

"Except that it's only nine thirty in the morning," she pointed out.

Right. Probably not going to find much champagne around Chatelaine this time of day.

"And I can't, because I'm pregnant," she added. "With twins."

Twins!

"Then we'll go to the Daily Grind and celebrate with coffee," he said.

"Except that I'm cutting back on caffeine."

"Did I say coffee? I meant herbal tea."

"Do you like herbal tea?"

"I hate it," he admitted. "But if you're cutting back on stuff for the sake of the baby's health, then I'll cut back in solidarity with you."

She smiled. "You don't have to do that."

"I know. But I want to. We're in this together, Sabrina. I mean it. Whatever I have to do to prove to you that we can do this fifty-fifty, I will. Even if it means drinking… What kind of herbal tea do you like?"

"Raspberry hibiscus."

Well, that sounded terrible.

"Even if it means drinking raspberry hibiscus tea," he told her. For the next six months. Dammit.

"Thanks, Zane."

He forced another smile. With any luck, the Daily Grind would be out of raspberry hibiscus tea. He threw the truck into gear and headed for the parking lot exit. It hit him as he stepped on the accelerator, though, that the two of them were embarking on a journey that would ultimately take them a lot farther than the Daily Grind. Just where they ended up, though...

Well, now. He kinda couldn't wait to find out.

Chapter Five

"What bad luck that they're out of raspberry hibiscus tea," Sabrina said as she and Zane took a seat at the back of the Daily Grind. "But what good luck that they had my second fave—ginger pomegranate."

"Yeah, that was lucky, all right," Zane replied.

Somehow, though, he didn't sound as happy to Sabrina about the development as she was. He reached for the sugar caddy and withdrew what looked like a dozen packets.

"It's actually kind of naturally sweet," she told him. "And all that sugar isn't really good for you."

He eyed her warily. "Are you telling me you're cutting back on sugar for the baby, too?"

She nodded. "I'm trying to cut it out completely. I gave the rest of the havreflarns to my mom."

Zane looked as happy about that as Sabrina had been. But, hey, sometimes you had to sacrifice for the greater good.

She lifted her unsweetened, but still sort of naturally sweet tea to her mouth to blow on it. "My mom said to tell you and Astrid thanks, by the way."

Zane nodded as, with clear reluctance, he returned the sugar packets to their caddy.

"And it's for the sake of the *babies*," she said. "Plural. We're having twins, remember?"

Even as she uttered the words, she still couldn't quite believe it. She had just gotten used to the idea of having *a* baby, and now she had to start all over again, getting used to the idea of having *two* babies. Two girls. Two. Twins. In case she hadn't mentioned that.

"The first girl Bastons in the family tree," Zane said.

Sabrina laughed lightly. "Look at you, bucking the family traditions and setting trends and bringing equality to the line."

He chuckled, too. "Yeah, but after raising a passel of boys, I don't have the first clue what I'm supposed to do with daughters."

"You raise girls the same way you raise boys, Zane. With love, respect and understanding."

He didn't look anywhere near convinced. Sabrina didn't blame him. Even if two babies didn't exactly constitute a passel, compared to the number of children she'd been planning on raising—namely, zero—it was a lot.

"It'll be fine," she tried to reassure him. Even if she hadn't quite reassured herself of that yet.

"I know," he said. "I do know that. It's just…" He inhaled a breath and released it slowly. "It's just a lot to take in."

She nodded. And they still hadn't worked out the specifics of their co-parenting. She knew they still had almost six months to make plans, but those months were going to fly by. February twenty-first. That was the projected due date for the twins if they went full term. But it was likely that they'd arrive early. Thirty-two to thirty-eight weeks instead of the usual forty. That was what Dr. Brewer had told her. Sabrina would follow every instruction to keep those babies in their protective womb as long as she could, but, when it came down to it, it wasn't entirely up to her. As her doctor had also told her, babies were gonna do what *they* wanted to do. And not just while they were in the womb, either.

Her head started to swim, and the room began to spin. She set her tea on the table, closed her eyes and leaned back in her chair to make it stop.

"You okay?" Zane asked.

She nodded.

"Can I get you anything?"

She shook her head.

"Maybe you should get something to eat. It's been a couple hours since breakfast. And you barely touched that. No wonder you look like you're about to faint."

"Thanks, Mom," she said.

He chuckled again. "That's *Dad* to you," he corrected her.

When she opened her eyes, she saw him looking at her with concern, in spite of his laughter.

"Seriously, maybe you need to eat," he told her. "All I saw were pastries at the counter. Do they have anything here that *isn't* sweet?"

"I doubt it."

"All right then. I'm taking you out for brunch."

"Zane, you don't have to do tha—"

"Oh, yes, I do. You're having Peach and Plum with a cattleman, Sabrina," he reminded her. As if she needed reminding of that, looking at the big Stetson sitting on the chair between them. "A cattleman whose baby girls are gonna grow up big and strong. So their mama is gonna need protein. Lots of it." He grinned. "Now finish up that tea you've been pretending to enjoy, and let's get outta here."

Zane's idea of going out for brunch, Sabrina discovered shortly after leaving the Daily Grind, actually meant going to his place for brunch. But she had to admit that the dish his housekeeper prepared for them on the fly, something made of eggs, bacon, tomatoes and chives, had been delicious. And so had the fried sausages she put on the side. Not to mention the smoked salmon and goat cheese on crispbread.

Scandinavians must like protein as much as cattlemen, she couldn't help thinking. Maybe she should come to Zane's house for brunch every morning. Or just spend the night beforehand so she didn't have to drive uncaffeinated, seeing as how that was super dangerous.

Then again, the ideas that were suddenly running through her head at the thought of spending the night here were even more dangerous. Because now all she could think about was that one night she did spend here with Zane. The one where they generated so much heat and so much passion and so much…oh, just *so much*… that they'd created a life together. *Two* lives.

Wow, was it getting hot in here? Damn those pregnancy hormones, anyway.

Before her thoughts could get away from her, Sabrina turned her attention back to the matter at hand. But the matter at hand mostly seemed to be how the two of them were now lingering in awkward silence at Zane's big dining room table over cups of the cloudberry tea Astrid had prepared for them from her own private stash. The housekeeper had been hovering over them like two children since Sabrina's arrival, so Zane had told her not to worry about cleaning up after them, that he would be fine clearing their plates and tidying up the kitchen himself.

"Now that was a proper meal," he said, finally breaking the silence as he leaned back in the big chair at the head of a gigantic table that was surrounded by a dozen other armless chairs like it. His was obviously the Head of the Household throne. His father had doubtless sat in that chair, too. And his grandfather. As well as his great-grandfather. And however many greats had come before them.

Like the rest of the house, the dining room was furnished in what Sabrina could only liken to a wealthy Spanish settlers' decor—most of it probably original to the house, too, she couldn't help thinking. Bare wood beams striped the ceiling that soared above them, and an enormous wrought-iron chandelier dangled over the table. The dark wood floor was spanned by wool rugs of varying sizes—from massive to less massive—decorated with complementary Native American designs, and all the furniture was big and dark and masculine, with lots of angles and sharp edges. They were going to have to do some serious toddler-proofing of his whole house before Peach and Plum were old enough to walk.

She tried to imagine two little girls sitting at the table opposite her, giggling over whatever they had most recently found funny. For some reason, they were fraternal twins in her mind's eye, one blond like her, the other brunette like Zane, but both having eyes that were a mix of her blue and his green. Mostly, though, she thought about how they would be swallowed up by the absolute bigness and unbridled masculinity of this house. Not that her log house was particularly small or feminine. But she'd done her best since moving in to soften and cozy it up as much as she could. It was a lot easier for her to imagine two little girls living in her house, with its smaller scale and curvy furniture, than she was seeing them here. How odd it was going to be for them to travel between two such contrary environments.

In how many other ways did she and Zane differ? she wondered. In what ways were the two of them going to clash when it came to raising their children? As much as they had talked about how they were going to be co-parenting, they still hadn't set up many guidelines for how they were going to go about it.

Where even now they should have been talking about their plans for the babies, they had instead spent the entirety of their meal talking about a million other things—Zane's family's history with Night Heron Ranch, Sabrina's hectic move to Chatelaine, the latest town gossip. It was painfully obvious that they were steadfastly avoiding the one subject they should have been focused on and instead ended their brunch talking about how many plans the Fortunes had for their newly acquired ranch. Which Sabrina couldn't help thinking made an obvious segue for something else they needed to talk about—her reasons for acquiring that adjacent plot of land she and Zane were at odds over.

"And then there's my textile camp," she said pointedly. "That's what I'm planning to put on that little piece of land I recently bought."

He eyed her knowingly. "But there are still some questions about the provenance of that land. It's not for certain that the sale to you was entirely legal. It's very possible it still belongs to my great-grandfather. And if that's the case, it's going to be out of play for you."

"It's mine," Sabrina told him. "Bought and paid for. My Realtor looked into the provenance, too, and said the sale your great-grandfather made was entirely legal, so the heirs were within their rights to sell it to me."

"But you still haven't closed," he reminded her. "Because there are still some potential provenance questions. And I'm going to need that property to water my cattle now that the pond on Night Heron Ranch is drying up."

"Ponds can be revived," she told him. "I read about it online. There are a lot of ways to do it. Have you looked into that?"

Because she had after Zane told her about his reasons for wanting the land, too, before leaving her house that night last week. Naturally, she didn't want his cattle to go without water. But even he had said that night that it was going to be inconvenient to drive his cattle that far from their usual grazing fields just to get them water every day. Ponds could be revitalized for relatively little cost and trouble. There was no reason he absolutely *had* to have that land.

"I have looked into it," he assured her. "And it's possible. But it's also time-consuming. And I think, in the long run, access to the lake from that bit of land is going to be the better alternative. Besides, you can put a textile camp anywhere."

"Not really. There aren't any small properties available besides that lakefront bit that's only a stone's throw from my house. That lakefront bit that I own."

"Not yet, you don't," he said. "Why do you need a textile camp anyway? Just what is a textile camp to begin with?"

"Exactly what it sounds like," she told him. "A camp for people to make things out of different kinds of fabrics and yarns. And to even learn to weave and spin textiles themselves." She shrugged. "I've loved to knit and crochet since I was a little girl, and I'm pretty handy with a sewing needle. My sister Dahlia is raising sheep on the Fortune ranch, so it makes sense for me to piggyback off of that. I'm going to try to convince her to add goats and maybe even alpacas at some point, too. Or see if Jade can have those in her petting zoo. The fibers from those animals are gorgeous. And I've always found working with textiles to be very therapeutic."

She hesitated, dropping her gaze to the table, then looked back up at him. "Especially when it comes to dealing with grief. That's what I'd like for this camp to be. A grief therapy camp for people who are trying to work through the loss of a loved one."

Zane studied her in thoughtful silence for a moment. Then, clearly choosing his words carefully, he said, "That first day, when you came here to tell me about the baby...*babies*," he quickly corrected himself, looking less panicky than he had since the sonogram, "you mentioned you were married before."

Heat detonated in the pit of Sabrina's belly. "I did? I don't remember that."

"Yeah, when you told me you'd changed your name to Fortune, and I thought you'd gotten married. You said you were never getting married again."

Oh, that's right. She remembered now. In the heat of the moment, she hadn't realized what she'd revealed. She'd never told anyone outside her family about her youthful marriage. She hadn't even told her family about it until she'd had to—after Preston's death, when she'd been so grief-stricken that she'd alarmed her parents and siblings to the point where they practically had to stage an intervention. Her father had been so angry about her relationship with a man who opposed him on every level and who he had been sure could only be interested in his daughter in order to get his hands on the Windham fortune, that Sabrina had been forced to see Preston in secret. She'd hidden their entire relationship, never mind the fact that they married.

"My husband's name was Preston," she told Zane without preamble. "We met and fell in love in high school. And he...he died. He died less than a year after we got married."

Zane said nothing for a moment. Then, very quietly, he told her, "I'm sorry, Sabrina. I didn't know."

"Of course you didn't. Hardly anyone does. I didn't even tell my sisters—who I tell *everything* to—that Preston and I got married. Not until after he passed away."

"Do you want to talk about it?"

She didn't. She hadn't talked about it to anyone for more than a decade. But for some reason, she felt like Zane had the right to know. And maybe sharing this with him would open up avenues to the two of them sharing other things. Things that would help them get to know each other better and maybe pave the way to talk about other important things. Things like how to parent two children neither of them had anticipated.

"My father didn't approve of the relationship," she began. "When Preston and I were still in high school, it was fine. Dad figured he was just my first boyfriend, young love and all that, someone I would naturally break up with in time and move on to someone else, the way teenagers often do."

"But you didn't break up," Zane guessed.

She shook her head. "We just got closer. And when Preston chose a biology major in college with a concentration on ecology and interned for an environmental watchdog agency that had my father's plastics company listed as public enemy number one in Texas... Well. Lead balloon and all that. Not to mention the fact that Preston was never going to make a fortune in life with his chosen profession, so that just convinced my father that he was only after the Windham money."

She smiled sadly and looked past Zane, out the window to where Night Heron Ranch sprawled off to the horizon. "Which is actually kind of funny when you think about it," she said softly. "Why would he want to put my father out of business if all he was after was my father's money? Anyway—" she hurried on, still not looking at Zane "—he died ten months after we married. An undiagnosed heart condition that was probably congenital." With much understatement, she concluded, "It hurt. A lot. I never want to go through that again. Not that I will, since I'm never going to fall in love again. The end."

When she met Zane's gaze again, it was to find him studying her in inscrutable silence, as if he were carefully weighing everything she'd just told him. His sea green eyes were deep and mesmerizing, and it was all Sabrina could do not to drown in them.

Finally, he said, "No offense, but I kinda sympathize with your father on the only-after-your-money thing." He lifted a hand when he saw her open her mouth to protest. "Not that that was the case with your husband," he said, to clarify. "I don't doubt he loved you as much as you loved him. I'm just talking from personal experience myself. I can see how a father would want to protect his daughter from that."

"What do you mean?" she asked.

"I mean I've had my fair share of gold diggers in the past," he told her. "Women who I eventually discovered were only interested in landing a rich husband."

"I think you're selling yourself short," Sabrina told him. "You have a lot more to offer a woman than money."

Oh, boy, was that an understatement. Any man with

gorgeous eyes like his, eyes that even now were smoky with wanting, and a sensuous mouth like his, a mouth that promised pleasures like no other, and corded, muscular arms like his, arms that could hold a woman with both gentleness and a passion that—

Um, anyway. He had a lot more to offer a woman than money.

He grinned at her comment, but it wasn't exactly a happy one. "Well, thank you for saying that, but too many women just see dollar signs when they look for a mate. Or maybe I just don't have the best judgment when it comes to women. Present company excluded, of course."

She smiled, too. "Thank *you* for saying that."

"But even at that, money wasn't enough for some women once they realized I was responsible for the care and feeding of my brothers. Guess they figured money goes fast when you have all those mouths to feed. Joke was on them, though. My parents set up trust funds for all five of us. We're all trust fund babies."

Sabrina chuckled. "Yeah, same here."

"Anyway, there were a handful of women who—" here he halted, as if he were trying to pick his words carefully "—okay, one in particular," he finally continued, "who got past the extra mouths and said it didn't matter. That the fact that I had stepped up to the plate to take care of my family made her love me even more. The boys loved her, too, after they met her. Which was a huge deal, since I never introduced any of my other girlfriends unless it got serious, and it almost never did." He exhaled roughly and a shadow crossed his face. "What

I didn't realize with this particular girlfriend was that she was just better than the others at hiding the fact that what she really loved was the Baston bank account. The day I went to her place to surprise her with a ring and a proposal, I overheard her through an open window on her phone. She had it on speaker and was talking to someone I later found out was her husband about how much money the two of them were going to pocket after she 'married' me and finagled a joint bank account."

Sabrina winced. She knew these things happened. She just wished *these things* hadn't happened to Zane.

"I'm sorry you went through that," she told him. "Clearly we both have excellent reasons for not wanting to get married."

He nodded. "We do."

She couldn't help smiling at the way he phrased his response. Once he realized what he'd done, he smiled, too.

"Okay, we *don't*," he amended. "But I'm still confident we can raise our children successfully, even without the gold bands and the piece of paper filed at the courthouse."

Sabrina hoped he was right. But she still couldn't ignore the fact that neither of them seemed to be in any hurry about how they were going to go about that. Why did they keep bringing up the fact that they needed to make a plan, then proceed to completely ignore the fact that they needed to make a plan?

She sighed. It was going to be a long gestation.

Zane and Sabrina didn't see each other for the next four days, since both had to do some catching up in other areas of their lives in the wake of all the sudden twin madness. And he had to admit, he was kind of grateful for the separation. Although they still had a lot of figuring out to do in the coming months—both individually and as co-parents—he reckoned they could both use some time to do the individual part before tackling the co-parent part again. Maybe the reason the two of them were having so much trouble talking about their expectations from each other was because they hadn't had time to think about their expectations of themselves. Co-parenting, he was already beginning to realize, was hard.

He was working in the barn when he was surprised by the arrival of his brother Cody, who was supposed to be a couple hundred miles away in Houston. He'd driven off with a Rice University sticker on the bumper of his car almost a week ago, wearing the blue-and-gray Rice T-shirt Zane had given him at his high school graduation. Classes started there five days ago. Cody was supposed to be neck deep in syllabi by now. Even more concerning, his youngest brother, who was just about the most happy-go-lucky kid Zane had ever known, looked super worried about something.

"What are you doing here?" he asked. "Is everything okay at school?"

Cody shook his head. "Not really, no."

"What's wrong?"

The kid looked even more worried. "I hate it, Zane."

"You've barely been there a week."

Zane told himself not to panic. It was understandable that his little brother wouldn't acclimate right away.

Being away from home was a huge adjustment, and Houston was a massive city compared to tiny Chatelaine. Hell, Zane himself had been homesick for a month when he first left home to go to Baylor. Cody would get past it. He just needed time.

"And I miss Hannah," his brother added.

And there it was. Zane told himself he shouldn't be surprised to hear Cody say that. He and his girlfriend had started dating when they were sophomores in high school and had been thick as thieves ever since, planning for their future together as only two teenagers could—completely oblivious to the realities of life. Hannah wasn't going to college—she'd turned her part-time job as a housekeeper into a full-time one at the Chatelaine Hills Hotel and Resort after graduation. They both loved horses, and they'd both talked about pursuing careers in rodeo work, because hey, being a rodeo cowboy and barrel racer were both such lucrative, steady careers that would make them rich and famous in no time. It had taken Zane nearly the entirety of Cody's senior year to talk him out of it and convince him to act on Rice's acceptance letter and generous financial package.

He'd assured his youngest brother that he and Hannah both had plenty of time to pursue rodeo work later if they still wanted to, confident that both kids would come to their senses after they'd had a few years to mature.

"Cody, we've talked about this," Zane reminded him. "College is such an amazing opportunity. It can open any door in life you want to open. If you end up deciding the rodeo is where you want to be, fine. But that can wait a few years while you explore other options."

Cody was shaking his head before Zane even finished talking. "I don't want other options, Zane," he said. "I want to join the rodeo. Hannah does, too."

Zane wanted to tell him it didn't matter what he wanted, that what their parents had wanted was for all five of the Baston boys to get a college education.

"You have to go to college," he insisted. "You need to get your tail back up to Houston right now. Otherwise, I'll hog-tie you and drive you back myself."

"Hannah and I are in love," he insisted. "I came back today because I can't bear to be apart from her."

Zane knew he had to choose his next words carefully. "It's great that you two are in love," he finally said. "Because love, real love, can get you through anything. Even four years of college."

He could tell Cody wanted to argue. He could practically feel the frustration radiating off his brother. He just hoped the kid's head won out over his heart.

Finally, Cody's shoulders slumped, and the challenge Zane had been fearing evaporated. "I hate it at school," he said softly.

"I get it," Zane told him. "I hated college at first, too. But then I loved it. Just give it time. You'll see." With much reluctance, he added, "And if you want to come back to visit Hannah on the weekends sometimes… *sometimes*," he said with emphasis, "your room at the house is always there."

Cody nodded and mumbled, "Okay."

Somehow, though, Zane knew it was going to be a while before anything with his youngest brother was okay. He told himself again that Cody just needed time.

The same way he and Sabrina did. Time could take care of a lot of problems, could straighten out a lot of things. All they needed—all of them—was a little more of that. And then everything—for all of them—would be okay.

Chapter Six

Sabrina hadn't visited her brother Ridge at his house since she first arrived in Chatelaine, and she was surprised at how far along he'd gotten with the place. Last time she was here, he still had some boxes to unpack, and all the furniture had been scattered helter-skelter until he could figure out how he wanted things done. He'd served her coffee in his travel mug and cookies straight out of the box. But now...

"Wow, this place has come a long way," she said as he closed the front door behind her. "It looks downright cozy in here."

And it really did. What could have been a masculine gray, brown and beige color palette was both brightened and softened by the addition of colorful accent touches, especially a vase of wildflowers sitting on one of the end tables. No way was Ridge responsible for those.

"I wish I could take the credit," he told her. He was dressed for an evening out on the town, nice jeans and a chocolate-colored polo that matched his dark hair and eyes. "But the truth is Hope has helped out a lot."

Sabrina made a quick survey to see if his mysterious houseguest was within earshot. Even seeing that she wasn't, she lowered her voice as she asked her brother, "How's she doing, anyway? You two have been kind of scarce lately."

"She and Evie are both fine, but I gotta admit neither of us still has any idea what her story is. Is she married? Is she running away from something? Or *someone*? Like the baby's father? I've scoured the internet looking for news about a missing woman and her baby, but there hasn't been anything. It's…worrying."

Sabrina nodded. The whole family was concerned. Even in the short time since she'd appeared in Chatelaine, all the Fortunes were becoming attached to Hope and her baby and were growing more apprehensive each day with what her past might hold.

"But yeah, sorry about the being-scarce part," Ridge added. "There's been a lot to do around here. It's been great having Hope's help putting it all together."

"Oh, I only helped, did I?"

Ridge had the decency to look sheepish as he turned to greet the woman with dark blond hair flecked with red in the light, who was striding into the living room cradling a baby against her shoulder. Her amber eyes were lit with teasing at Ridge's comment. Even so, Sabrina could detect an air of distance in her, as if Hope was still wary around the man who'd discovered her. Not that Sabrina blamed her. She couldn't imagine not knowing the facts of one's own life. Of course Hope would be wary around them.

"Okay, she's pretty much responsible for how nice the place looks," Ridge told his big sister. To Hope, he added, "Did you manage to get some sleep?"

"A little," she said. "Enough to get me through the evening, anyway."

Sabrina had come over tonight because Ridge had asked her to babysit so that he and Hope could get a little time to themselves, away from the demands of an infant. She had jumped at the chance both because she hadn't seen Hope or Evie for a while, but also to get in a little baby practice for herself. Sabrina had never really been around kids much in spite of working for a children's charity when she lived in Dallas, and she for sure had never been around babies before. She figured tonight would give her a little intro into what she and Zane had coming.

While Sabrina had only met Hope a handful of times, it was clear as she strode across the living room that the woman had come a long way, too, in the weeks since she'd shown up on the ranch. The superficial injury to her head that she'd had that night Ridge and Dahlia found her in his barn had healed, and she didn't look as haunted as she had during those first days. Her eyes were no longer shadowed by strain, and her hair was caught at her nape in a tidy braid. Blue-eyed Evie strongly resembled her mother, right down to the highlights in the downy hair sticking up on her head and the star-shaped birthmark mother and daughter both had on their necks. She was dressed in a daisy-spattered sleeper and looked like she'd doubled in size since the last time Sabrina had seen her.

"Holy moly, what are you guys feeding this baby?" she asked with a chuckle as she went to greet her charge for the night.

"Right?" Ridge said. "Babies are amazing. Sometimes she seems like she's bigger in the morning than she was when we put her to bed the night before. Evie's changed even faster than this house has."

"But there's still plenty to do around here," Hope said. "A lot left to unpack. It'll be Christmas before this place is in shape."

"Yeah, if we ever even *find* the Christmas stuff," he grumbled good-naturedly.

Sabrina smiled down at Evie, and when the baby smiled back, a ribbon of delight unwound inside her. "She smiled at me!" she cried as she looked up at Ridge and Hope again. "She likes me!"

"Of course she likes you," Hope told her. "You're a big sweetheart. You're going to be a great mom, Sabrina."

Sabrina wished that statement would make her happy, too, but instead, a curl of anxiety coiled up tight inside her. Some of that was her concern that she didn't know the first thing about mothering, but some of it was twisted up with Zane, too. Talk about not knowing what she was doing.

She hadn't seen him for days, but it felt more like months had passed since their brunch at his ranch. And not a single one of those days had gone by without her thinking about him. A lot. There were times when she could almost convince herself that everything between the two of them would work out fine—eventually. But there were other times when she wondered if they would ever be able to free the knots in their relationship.

"I hope you're right," she said. "I feel so clueless."

And not just about the baby. But if she started telling Ridge and Hope about everything that was going on with her and Zane, they'd never get out the front door to enjoy their evening.

"You'll learn as you go, just like every other new parent," Hope assured her. "Really. It'll be fine."

As if to punctuate that, Evie lifted a pudgy little hand to wrap her fingers around one of Sabrina's, then cooed in a way that made her feel as if Hope was right, and that everything would be fine. *Eventually.*

"So how have you been, Hope?" Sabrina asked. "Have you been able to remember anything about your past?"

She shook her head sadly. "No, but I've been having some weird dreams."

"Like what?"

"It's of two people. I can't see their faces—it's all a blur—but I can tell they're an older couple. And in the dreams, I seem to know them."

"Well, that's encouraging. Do they say anything?"

Another head shake, then Hope told her, "They both reach out for me, and at first, that's really comforting, and it makes me feel happy in the dream. But then I suddenly realize that they're angry about something. Are they angry at me? Angry about something I've done or said? Are they people from my past? Or is it all just a bizarre dream that doesn't mean anything? I don't have any idea."

"Well, it sounds to me like your brain is trying to work things out," Sabrina said gently. "That's something."

"I suppose."

"But tonight, we're not going to worry about any

of that," Ridge interjected. "We're just going to have a nice dinner at the LC Club, then take a walk along the lakefront, maybe stop for ice cream at some point, and just relax."

Hope smiled. "Relaxing. What a concept!"

"Evie, listen to them," Sabrina cooed to the baby. "Talking like you're a lot of trouble. I don't believe them for a minute. You're just the sweetest, cutest, bestest baby in the whole wide world."

At least until mine come along, she added to herself. *They're going to give you a run for your money in the sweet and cute and best department. Right, Peach and Plum?* she added to the twins growing inside her. *You're going to be sweet, aren't you? Right?*

As if they heard her inner dialogue loud and clear, Hope and Ridge both chuckled.

"Yeah, babies are a breeze, Sabrina," Ridge said with a mischievous smile. "Just you wait. You'll have nothing but time on your hands after those little bundles arrive."

"Yeah," Hope agreed. "And you'll feel so well rested. All the time. Really. You will."

Sabrina eyed them both warily. They didn't seem like they were being quite honest. Hmm…

"Hey, would you guys mind if I invited Zane over tonight for a little bit?" she asked them. "Just so, you know, he could get some hands-on baby experience, too?"

Now her companions' smiles turned knowing. "Oh, so he can get some *baby experience*," Ridge echoed.

"Yeah, it could have nothing to do with those dreamy blue eyes of his, could it?"

"Of course not," Sabrina was quick to deny. Zane had green eyes after all. But a frisson of heat shot through her all the same. "I just think he'd welcome the chance to spend a little time with Evie, too, that's all."

"Gotcha," Ridge said. Still smiling his smug-brother smile.

"Of course we don't mind," Hope said. "Zane seems like a good guy."

"Thanks," Sabrina told them. "You guys have fun tonight. Don't worry about a thing. Zane and I will have a nice relaxing night here with Evie."

When Sabrina had invited Zane to come over to her brother's house where she was babysitting a literal baby, Zane had envisioned the two of them having a fun night with the little bundle of joy. Tummy time on the floor, like he'd been reading about, with him on one side of Evie and Sabrina on the other, while they watched the baby coo and laugh and reach for squishy toys. Or holding her in his lap while he read her one of those cute little board books he'd seen at Remi's Reads the other day. And, okay, bought a couple, too. Or maybe doing that *Open your mouth, here comes the choo-choo train* feedings where he chugged a spoonful of strained prunes into the little girl's mouth.

What he *hadn't* anticipated was thirty straight minutes of crying for no reason that he or Sabrina could find a cause for.

"Here, let me try, again," he said when Sabrina's gentle bobbing up and down of her body and soft words didn't calm the baby down.

She happily turned Evie over to him, and Zane began walking in slow circles around the room, murmuring nonsense words into the baby's ears. For a moment, her crying did ease up some—maybe because there was a new voice in her ear. But after a moment, she went right back to howling again.

"I don't understand what we're doing wrong," Sabrina told him. "She's been fed. Her diaper's fine. She doesn't seem to be hurt. Is she maybe scared of something? Scared of us?"

"She wasn't scared of us earlier," Zane pointed out.

In fact, she'd seemed to like them both at first. Little Evie had been fascinated by Zane's Stetson when he came in, and she'd laughed when he took it off, as if she hadn't expected that to happen and was delighted by the surprise. He and Sabrina had both held her and sat with her on their laps, talking to her and having her respond with her little baby *oohs* and *aahs* and gurgles and spit. Which Zane hadn't even minded on account of it was cute spit.

Then, out of nowhere, she'd just started crying. Even screaming at times. A lot.

"Maybe she just misses her mommy," Sabrina said.

Her expression suddenly changed, and she moved to the chair where she'd left her purse. She withdrew her phone from the side pocket and started scrolling. "Hang on," she added. "I still have a voicemail from Hope with some pointers."

She pressed Play, nudged up the volume and Hope's voice sounded even louder than the baby's crying. It took a few seconds for the sound to register with Evie, but when it did, her crying stopped. Immediately. Sabrina turned down the sound to a more normal volume, and Hope's voice listing mundane facts about feeding time, favorite book, favorite song, where to find clean jammies, etcetera droned from the speaker. She might as well have been telling Evie that Santa Claus was coming to town, so happy did the baby become by the simple sound of her mother's voice.

"Unbelievable," Zane said as he continued to study the baby and gently rock her. "All she wanted was to know her mommy is still around."

"I guess that's pretty important when Mommy is your entire world."

Now he snapped up his head to look at Sabrina. "Wow. I never thought about it like that. From the babies' points of view, we're going to be *everything*. They're not going to be aware of anything but us for a while. That kind of adds a whole 'nother level of pressure, doesn't it?"

He could tell by Sabrina's responding expression that she hadn't thought about that until now, either. *Great. They could panic together.*

"If we're not careful with the twins," she said, "we could turn them into serial killers."

He chuckled at that. "Or we could turn them into the people who will bring world peace."

"Yeah, I like that better," she told him.

Hope's recording came to an end, and the baby started to fret once more. So Zane told Sabrina to hit the play button again. When she did, Evie went back to happy, even smiling, at the sound of her mother's voice.

They continued to hit replay for another ten minutes, until Evie opened her mouth in the biggest yawn Zane had ever seen.

"I think somebody's finally starting to get sleepy," he said softly.

"Here, let me take her," Sabrina said. "Hope mentioned her favorite song is 'You Are My Sunshine.' It's guaranteed to put her out like a light. I know my voice isn't like Hope's, but maybe it will be close enough."

Zane knew that about the song. On account of he'd just heard Hope say it in her recording a dozen times. But Sabrina was right. The baby was more likely to be lulled by a woman's voice singing her a lullaby than a man's. He handed the baby back to her—feeling oddly bereft once the little bundle was out of his grasp—then followed her to the baby's nursery upstairs.

Which, he couldn't help noticing upon arrival, was almost better furnished than his own bedroom. It was cozier, too. And far more welcoming. Hell, Zane was halfway ready to crawl into the crib and grab a few z's himself.

"Dang," he said. "Hope and Ridge went all out for Evie, didn't they?"

Sabrina nodded. "And they did it fast. It's adorable, isn't it?"

A soft white-and-beige background held pops of green, all of it inspiring a feeling of calmness and serenity. There were stuffed animals everywhere he looked—probably courtesy of Ridge, since Hope and Evie, Zane knew, thanks to all the gossip in town, had shown up in Chatelaine with literally just the clothes on their backs. It was the perfect room for a growing baby. Sabrina had told him how her little brother had taken mother and child under his wing, but Zane had had no idea the extent that had happened. Looked to him like Ridge was planning for something of an extended stay for the two.

"You know," he told Sabrina as she made her way toward a rocking chair in the corner, "you and I probably ought to start thinking about putting together a room in our houses, too, for the twins. I mean, I know we still have five or six months before they're here, but I guess it's never too early to start planning."

She sat down with Evie cradled in her lap and started rocking to soothe the baby's fretting. "I've thought about that, too," she said, "but I just haven't had much time to really do anything concrete. You're right, though. If we put it off too long, our babies are going to be sleeping in milk crates. There aren't a lot of baby outlets in Chatelaine, though. Or, you know, even one baby outlet in Chatelaine. I know the GreatStore probably has stuff, but I'd really like to compare different places."

"Maybe we can make a trip to Corpus Christi next week," he offered. "Surely they have a lot of baby places there."

She smiled. "I'd like that."

She looked like she was going to say more, but Evie began to fuss again, so she turned her attention to the baby. Zane switched off the overhead light, leaving the room bathed in the soft glow of a moon-shaped nightlight near the crib, just enough light to see where everything was, but not enough to disturb sleep. Sabrina began to hum the melody to the song Hope had said was Evie's favorite, then she started to sing, her voice as soft and gentle as a well-loved blankie. Evie quieted immediately, making those dainty little cooing sounds Zane had found so delightful when he first heard them.

He really didn't have any experience with babies. Nada. None of his friends had procreated yet, and his family members were all either too young to have any or too far-flung to share their offspring. Evie was so little. And according to Sabrina, she was already around four months old. Just how small were Peach and Plum going to be when they were born? Especially since he'd heard twins often arrived early. How was he supposed to handle two tiny little human beings who were completely vulnerable? His daughters would be dependent on him for everything for years. He would be their first line of protection from all the bad things in the world.

Nobody knows, dear, how much I love you...

As he listened to Sabrina sing to the baby, something inside Zane swelled almost too big for him to hold it. Something fierce and enormous and scary. It was all he could do to rein it in before it overwhelmed him completely.

He knew in that moment that he would do whatever he had to do to make sure his girls stayed safe and healthy and happy. And not just his daughters— their mother, too. He wasn't sure what all this...*stuff* was that was mushrooming inside him, but he knew it wasn't going to go away. He knew it was only going to get stronger. And he knew it was going to take some time before he figured it all out. But yeah—it was never going to go away. That much he did know.

By now, Evie had nodded off, and Sabrina was standing slowly and carefully to carry her to her crib. She settled the baby gently onto the mattress, switched on the baby monitor hanging on the side, then turned to look at Zane. She covered her mouth with her index finger, then tiptoed melodramatically to the door where he was standing. But the smile she'd been wearing faltered some when she drew close enough to get a good look at him.

"What's wrong?" she whispered.

"Nothing," he told her just as softly. "Nothing is wrong."

"You look like someone just told you the world is ending."

He shook his head. "No, not at all. Just the opposite, actually. I think I just realized the world is only now about to begin. A new world, anyway. One unlike anything I've ever known before."

She studied him in silence for a moment, then nodded. "I think I know what you mean," she said. "Everything is going to be different once Peach and Plum arrive."

He wanted to tell her everything was different *now*. But if he said that, she'd want to know what he meant. And truth was, Zane honestly didn't know. He wasn't sure what to think at the moment. All he knew to do right now was feel. And what he felt…

What he felt was indescribable.

So he only replied, "Yeah. It will be. So you and I better get on the stick and make some of those plans we keep talking about but never talk about."

"Later this week," she promised. "Whatever day you

have free. Let's go to Corpus Christi. It's time you and I finally started making our nests for the two little chicks who will be hatching before long."

Chapter Seven

"Zane, everything doesn't have to be pink and lavender."

It was the third time Sabrina had made the comment, since this was the third store she and Zane had visited since coming to Corpus Christi after making their decision to shop for the nurseries in their respective homes. Chatelaine wasn't teeming with home improvement stores any more than it was baby boutiques, and they'd been looking for paint and such, too.

Corpus Christi, on the other hand, had a lot of specialty shops and boutiques dedicated specifically to child-related environments ranging from indoor to outdoor, with every theme under the sun. She just wished Zane would stop gravitating toward the same theme over and over again. They'd started in the paint store, where he'd gone straight to the pastels—specifically, the traditionally girly pastels. At the baby furniture store, he'd wandered toward all things white and frilly, specifically a couple of cribs with pink and lavender canopies. Now they were at one of those everything-a-baby-could-need superstores, and he had his gaze trained on a stuffed unicorn with a skimpily clad fairy on its back.

"In fact," she added, "I'd prefer if we just avoided gender specific colors entirely." It was the third time she'd told him that, too. This time, though, she backed it up with solid research. "Baby nurseries need a variety of different colors, regardless of whether that baby is a boy or a girl. Colors that are bright and gender neutral and provide a great contrast to each other, since brightness and contrast are what you want when a baby's vision is developing."

"Says who?" Zane wanted to know.

"Says all the baby books and blogs I've been reading," she told him.

All three of them. That she'd quickly scanned last night in preparation for this shopping excursion. Not that she mentioned that part to Zane.

"Besides, not every girl loves pink and lavender," she said. Again. He started to reach for the fairy-riding unicorn. "And not all of them love unicorns and fairies."

He pulled his hand back. Then he hooked both hands on his hips in challenge. "Yeah, well, after raising four boys, you'll forgive me if I'm a little excited about having some girls in the family," he told her. "Maybe I want to go a little overboard with the girly stuff."

Okay, she could see that. But having worked for too long in a male-dominated world—and having never exactly been a girly-girl herself—Sabrina still balked at introducing someone else's ideas of what they specified as girl- or boy-centered items. Sheesh. Every store they'd visited had actually had departments devoted to gender.

"Let's just stick to the basics until we know what's going to spark Peach's and Plum's interests," she said.

"Bright, contrasting colors. And animals. Kids of all kinds love animals."

In spite of their little disagreement, Zane smiled. "You really want that Noah's ark quilt we saw when we came in, don't you?"

Okay, yeah, she did. It was the cutest thing she'd ever seen. But that wasn't why she'd brought up animals. She just appreciated excellent craftsmanship when she saw it, that was all.

"I just think it will go great with the four different colors I'm going to paint the nursery at my house— each one bright and contrasting." Okay, kind of bright, she amended. A little. Okay, fine, they were all in the pastel family. She just liked softer colors. So sue her. But they *were* all gender neutral. And they *did* contrast. "And now I'm thinking about hiring an artist to paint a cute mural of an island full of animals on one of the walls in there. What are you thinking for the nursery at your house?"

Judging by his expression, he either hadn't given any thought to that at all, or he knew she was going to dislike the ideas he had been entertaining.

"You were going with unicorns and fairies, weren't you?"

"No." He denied it in a way that told her that had been exactly his plan. That was only reinforced when he added, "I mean, I do live on a ranch, Sabrina. And unicorns are horses. Sorta."

"Well, there you go," she told him, pretending she had no idea he'd been going for the gender stereotype.

"Horses. Ranch. Why not put a ranch theme in there? With horses?" *That* aren't *unicorns*, she added to herself.

He frowned. "Right. A ranch theme for a baby nursery. I'll just line the walls with creekstone, hang some mounted longhorns over cribs made out of fence posts and barbwire, and throw a big ole cowhide rug on the floor. Decorate with a few saddles and branding irons, and it'll be the perfect room for my baby girls."

She knew he was being hyperbolic on purpose, but she said, "Hey, they might want to take over their father's ranch business when they're old enough, you never know. That would go a long way toward preparing them."

He glared at her.

"I'm just saying you could do some cute little baby cows and ponies and maybe some chicks and ducklings and—"

"I don't raise poultry, Sabrina," he bit out.

"Yeah, but Peach and Plum won't know that."

He dropped his hands from his hips but did at least move away from the unicorn. "You know what? Wyatt's an art major. I think I'll just consult with him on this."

Well, that was certainly promising. Sabrina perked up even more. If his brother was an artist, then maybe…

"Would he possibly be up for a commission to paint a mural in his nieces' nursery at my place?" she asked.

Zane laughed. "Hell, he'd probably pay you to let him do it. Those boys are already fighting over who's going to be the coolest uncle."

Sabrina laughed. "They'll have to get in line. My brothers are having the same argument."

Zane sighed heavily. "A ranch theme might work," he

conceded. "Wyatt could probably do something really nice with that. But no chicks or ducklings or anything else. Just cows and horses."

She was going to throw in a bid for lambs, too, since Dahlia was raising sheep, but she didn't push her luck. However, she made a mental note to bring it up later, when he was in a better mood.

Instead, she only suggested, "Let's see if they have anything here that might jump-start that on your end of things." Because she was for sure getting those Noah's ark quilts.

Funnily, the shop did have some cute accessories for a ranch nursery. Zane bought two baby quilts spattered with cartoon cowgirls, some sheets decorated with horseshoes and two little armoires that opened with what looked like minuscule barn doors.

"There," he said when they finally made it to the checkout counter. "Let's see what Wyatt can do with those."

Hopefully find a rug and some prints that would tie it all together, Sabrina thought. Not that she didn't have her own work cut out for her since yes, she'd only found a few things that would work with the Noah's ark quilts. But at least she had the rug, one with two entwined giraffes that was also just about the cutest thing she'd ever seen. And if she could pay Uncle Wyatt to paint a couple of murals in the girls' room, she wouldn't need more than a few prints for the other walls.

They paid and arranged for delivery of their purchases for the following afternoon, then Zane looked at his watch. "Wow. This took a lot longer than I thought it would. It's almost dinnertime. Are you hungry?"

Was she hungry? Sabrina echoed to herself. She was pregnant with twins. *Of course* she was hungry. She didn't think she was going to stop being hungry until after they were born.

"I could definitely eat," she told him as they made their way out of the store and into the balmy evening.

The sun was dipping low above the buildings, but the pedestrian traffic on the sidewalk was still brisk. Zane looked one way up the street, then down the other, then back at Sabrina. A couple walking by brushed him softly, so he took a step closer to her to move outside the throng of passersby.

"I've only been to Corpus Christi a few times," he told her, "so I'm not all that familiar with the restaurant scene. How about you?"

She shook her head. "I don't think I've been here since I was a little girl. My folks used to bring us here for vacation sometimes. Well, Mom mostly. Dad would stay for a day or two, then fly home because he had business to attend to."

"I'm sure we can find something. What are you in the mood for?" Zane asked.

Mexican, Sabrina decided immediately. No, Mediterranean. No, wait, Indian. Maybe Italian? Or Chinese? But then, good ole fried chicken and corn on the cob sounded good, too. Maybe all of the above...?

Wow, their daughters already had really eclectic tastes in cuisine.

"Um, I'm open for anything?" she said with much understatement. Zane would probably be way better at narrowing things down than she was, since he currently only had one stomach inside his body. "What sounds good to you?"

"Steak," he answered immediately. "Steak always sounds good to me. I'm gonna go out on a limb, though, and guess that red meat isn't great for someone who's pregnant."

Sabrina shook her head sadly. "I'm supposed to cut back on red meat consumption. But we can go someplace that has steak and other stuff."

Zane shook his head, too. "Nah. I'm in this with you. If you can't have a big ole bloody steak, then I'm not having one, either."

"Zane, you really don't have to make the same sacrifices I am for this pregnancy. Especially since, you know, cattle. Beef. It's kind of your thing."

"Yes, I do have to make the same sacrifices," he replied. "But after those girls are born, you're coming to Night Heron Ranch, and I'm going to grill you the best steak you've ever had."

She smiled. "It's a date." When she realized how badly she'd misspoken, she quickly corrected herself. "I mean, that sounds like fun. Thanks."

Too late, though. Even with the correction, she was definitely thinking about dates with Zane. And not just the one that had ended with the twins' conception, the memory of which sent a sizzle of heat shimmying down her spine. But also the potential for other dates with him in the future. Which she shouldn't be thinking about at all, because dates meant there would be more to their relationship than co-parenting, and there totally would *not* be more to their relationship than co-parenting, sizzling spine notwithstanding.

She could tell by his expression that Zane had noticed her slip, too, and that his thoughts now were mirroring her own. At least the ones about remembering their first date together. His eyes darkened as his gaze fixed on hers for a moment, then he dropped it lower to focus on her mouth. His lips parted fractionally, and he seemed to lean in a little. Without even realizing she was doing it, Sabrina leaned in, too. Closer and closer they drew to each other, until she could feel his heat joining with her own. Then someone hurrying by them bumped Zane's shoulder and uttered a quick apology before moving on. It was enough to bring them both back to the present, and they pulled apart, each suddenly becoming way more interested in the comings and goings of Corpus Christi than they were in each other.

"Um…so…" Sabrina stammered, not even sure what she intended to say.

"Yeah…so…" Zane agreed just as vaguely.

She reminded herself they'd been talking about dinner and was about to ask him again what he was in the mood for. Then she realized what a loaded question that would be in light of the last few moments and tried again.

"We passed a restaurant up the street near where we parked," she said. "It looked like one of those places that serves a lot of different things. I wouldn't think it would be that busy on a weeknight."

Zane nodded, but still looked as confused by their sudden shifts in mood as Sabrina was. Even so, "Sounds perfect," he said.

* * *

And it was. Sabrina ordered a few things from the appetizer menu to cover as many of her cravings as she could, and Zane, after reluctantly reading the descriptions of the steaks, opted for pork chops, which Sabrina decided not to tell him were technically considered red meat, too, despite the "other white meat" ad campaign, since he'd been so good about sacrificing so many other things.

He really was going to be a good father, she thought. Not just because he already had experience with it via his brothers, but because he was just such a decent human being. Someone who understood the big picture, that it wasn't always about one person, and that you sometimes had to make sacrifices in order to secure the well-being of others. Sabrina was already understanding that that, really, was what good parenting came down to. Her life wasn't just hers anymore. She had others to think about now. Because two little babies, who would become two little kids then grow into two adolescents, would be vulnerable. They would need someone not to just care for them and make sure they were clothed and fed and educated, but someone to watch out for them, too. Someone to have their backs. Someone who would always—always—put them first.

And it wasn't just their babies, Sabrina knew, that Zane would do all those things for. He would do them for her, too. Somehow she knew that to the depth of her soul. Probably because she realized she felt the same way about him. He was the father of her children. Of course she would do whatever she had to do to keep him safe and healthy and happy.

And she made herself admit that, on some level, she would do all those things because Zane was becoming important to her for other reasons, too. Reasons that had nothing to do with the twins and everything to do with her. And with him. And with them. She just wasn't quite ready yet to explore why, exactly, that was. There were just too many feelings tying together inside her lately that she wasn't sure yet where to begin unknotting them.

They took their time as they ate, talking about even more things they hadn't yet considered when it came to the babies. They needed to start interviewing pediatricians. Looking into day care—or decide if they would even send their babies to day care. It was entirely possible that between the two of them and their families, they already had that covered. Sabrina knew she could take the girls to work with her, but she wasn't sure how difficult it might be to juggle her responsibilities for Fortune Ranch with not one but two infant schedules. Once they were old enough to be out and about, Zane said, they could tag along with him for some of his ranch chores. He even offered to talk to Astrid about taking on some childcare duties in exchange for a hefty salary raise.

And schooling. Would Chatelaine's sole preschool be a good fit for the girls? And what about the town's only elementary, middle and high schools? They were going to need to look into those, too, and especially tour the preschool if they wanted to get on the waiting list there. Chatelaine seemed to be bursting with babies lately, what with all the newcomers to town and weddings and procreation going on as a result.

They spent so much time talking over dinner that

neither realized just how late it was getting until they looked up to find they were the only diners left in the place. Zane asked for the bill, apologized to their server for overstaying when she brought it, then laughed in Sabrina's face when she told him she wanted to pay her share.

"Next time's on me then," she told him as he signed the receipt.

"We'll talk about that next time," he told her.

Next time, she repeated to herself. The handful of times she'd dated since her husband's death, the words *next time* hadn't come up a whole lot. She just hadn't felt much chemistry with those men. Which, she supposed, was another reason things had happened so quickly with Zane that night. The chemistry she'd felt with him had been nothing short of… Well, whatever branch of chemistry was most explosive. The thought that there would be a string of *next times* with him now made her remember what happened on the sidewalk earlier in light of her similar thoughts. And that sent a thrill of something hot and electric zinging through her like a live wire.

She tried to tell herself the only reason for any *next times* with Zane in the foreseeable future would be because the two of them were co-parenting the babies growing inside her. There was no reason for hot and electric. No reason for zinging. No reason for live wires. Unfortunately, she couldn't quite convince herself of that.

"We better get going if we want to be back in Chatelaine before bedtime," Zane told her.

She looked at her watch. It was already *past* her bedtime. Pregnancy had sapped her in a way she didn't know was possible. She used to be such a night owl. But she couldn't remember the last time she'd gone to bed after ten. Doubtless, she would be taking a nap on the way home.

Unfortunately, getting some shut-eye on the drive home didn't happen because they saw the entry ramp onto the interstate was barricaded by a police car. When Zane checked his phone to find out why, it was to discover that all eastbound lanes were blocked until morning thanks to an overturned semi that had spilled its entire load of soybean oil all over the road.

"Well, that's not good," he said unnecessarily.

"What about alternate routes?" Sabrina asked. "There's got to be more than one way from Corpus Christi to Chatelaine."

"There is," he told her. "But too much of it is two-lane country roads that I'm not familiar with at all. And I learned my lesson as a teenager that back roads in Texas in the middle of the night can be more than a little dangerous." He met her gaze levelly. "When you're a kid and don't know any better, you feel immortal enough not to care. But we're not kids, and we have more than ourselves to think about now." His gaze dropped to her lap. "I'm not willing to take any risks with the precious cargo you're carrying."

"I appreciate that, Zane," she said. "And I agree. But that does leave us with a bit of a problem. We can't sleep in your truck."

He chuckled. "No worries. We'll just get a couple hotel rooms for the night."

Except that that was a problem, too, they soon found

out, thanks to a major tech convention that was going on all week. Zane and Sabrina both spent the next thirty minutes parked and scrolling through their phones to find accommodations. But every hotel they checked was booked solid. Until finally, they found one a half-hour outside the city proper.

"Here's one," she said. "But yikes. It's called the Rendezvous Motel. Not sure I like the sound of that. That sounds like the kind of place that books rooms by the hour."

Zane brought up a travel site to check it out. "It's actually got decent reviews. It's an old place from the fifties, but it sounds like it's clean and family friendly."

"They only have one room left," Sabrina said. Even so, she tapped the *Reserve now* button before it was gone, too. She put down her phone. "But it's a double," she told him. "So we should be okay."

Sabrina didn't relax, though, until they arrived at the Rendezvous Motel and saw that it was adorable, a relic of the mid-twentieth-century motor lodge culture that had been lovingly restored to its original, well, adorableness. Lots of turquoise paint. And potted cacti. Not to mention a ton of pink and green neon.

But only one bed, they discovered when they checked in to claim their room. The desk clerk—who looked original to the place, too, with her puff of white hair and beaded-flower cardigan and cat-eye glasses—told them they were *super* lucky to find it, since the previous reservation for it had been canceled less than an hour before Sabrina booked it. And good thing there was only two of them, otherwise someone would be sleeping on the floor, since they were all out of cots, too.

"There's only one bed?" Sabrina asked in reply to the clerk's comment. "But the listing said it was a double room."

"Right. Double room. One double bed."

"No, double room means two beds."

The desk clerk was clearly surprised by this. "Since when?"

"Since always."

"Huh. Gonna have to look into that. Anyway, payment up front. Please and thank you. Sign here."

Sabrina looked helplessly at Zane, who shrugged his concurrence with her confusion as he handed the clerk his credit card. What were they supposed to do? his expression said. There was nowhere else for them to stay, and there would be no driving home tonight.

The receptionist at least had a couple of essential toiletries kits to give them, so they could brush their teeth and such, and there was breakfast provided in the morning, she told them. Then Zane and Sabrina were left to their own devices—and a room with only one bed.

One *full-size* bed that seemed way tinier than the queen she had at home. The whole room was tiny— if charmingly furnished like something out of a road trip movie starring Doris Day and Rock Hudson—right down to the bathroom that was hardly big enough for a person to turn around.

"I'll sleep in the tub," Zane told her.

"Are you kidding?" she said. "A toddler couldn't sleep comfortably in that tub."

"Then I'll sleep on the floor."

She expelled an errant sound. "Look, we can both sleep in the bed," she said. "We're adults. And, hey, we've shared a bed before."

Of course, look how that had turned out. They'd created life not once but twice the last time they shared a bed. Still, there was little chance of that happening again, was there?

Then she remembered their near-kiss on the sidewalk a matter of hours ago, and all the heat and sizzle that had accompanied it. Heat and sizzle that were still shimmering just beneath the surface and trying to bubble their way back to the top.

"It'll be fine," she told him. Almost convincingly, too.

It *would* be find, she assured herself more forcefully. She was half-asleep already. It had been a long day. They could just brush their teeth, fall into bed and they'd be out like a light in no time. By tomorrow morning, with any luck, the highway would no longer be a menace, and they could zip right back to Chatelaine. At worst, they could take the side roads in full daylight and make it home just the same.

A good night's sleep. That was what they both needed. And there was absolutely no reason to think that wasn't what the two of them would get.

Zane woke slowly, not sure at first where he was, because in some dusty corner of his brain, he was pretty sure he wasn't in his own bed. That bed was king-size, with plenty of room for a man to spread out—and he did like to spread out when he slept—while this one was small and crowded. Crowded because he was pretty sure he wasn't alone. That was another dead giveaway that this wasn't his bed, because he hadn't woken up with another person since… Well, he'd been about to think since that night with Sabrina, but she'd left before dawn, so he'd been alone that morning, too.

This morning, though, he felt a warm, soft body pressed affectionately against his own. In fact, this body was entwined with his, from the slender leg looped over his own from behind him to the graceful arm draped possessively around his waist to the silky head tucked into the crook of his neck.

This had to be a dream. A really good one, too. One he didn't quite want to end. So he snuggled more intently into his pillow and—what the hell, it was his dream—reached behind himself to drape his arm over the body behind his. When he did, he heard a soft sigh, then felt his companion push herself more intimately against him. Then he felt the hand at his waist move up over his chest, splaying open over his heart. Which, it went without saying, began to beat more rapidly. Instinctively, eyes still closed—since he was dreaming after all—he turned to his other side to face his imaginary partner, only to have her curl up even closer to him. Her mouth went to his neck, and she brushed her lips against the sensitive skin there before dragging a few kisses along the line of his jaw and back again.

Zane responded by turning his head so that his mouth covered hers, kissing her once, twice, three times, before skimming his hand down her back to cover her fanny. In turn, she deepened their kiss and pulled him closer, crowding herself into the cradle of his thighs. He sprang to life at the contact, moving his body again so that she was flat on her back beneath him. For long moments, he and his dream woman vied for possession of the kiss, until she sighed against his neck and murmured, *"Oh, Zane"* in a voice that sounded really, really familiar. That was when it finally dawned on him that, well, maybe he wasn't dreaming after all.

He opened his eyes at the same time Sabrina did, and both of them immediately stopped what they were doing. Which left her with her fingers twined intimately in his hair, him affectionately cupping her, ah, derriere, and both of them gazing at each other in complete disbelief and mortification.

"I was dreaming," she said vehemently.

"So was I," he assured her just as quickly.

She nibbled her lower lip. Zane tried not to help her. "I mean… I *thought* I was dreaming," she said.

"Same here."

It took another minute—another minute where Zane just wanted to stay in bed like this forever—before it occurred to either of them to disengage. And then they did so with all the speed and propulsion of an Indy 500 racer. Zane moved to one side of the bed and slung his feet over to the floor while Sabrina fled to the other side and did likewise. A long moment passed before either of them spoke again, and when they did, it was to speak at the same time.

"That shouldn't have happened."

"That was a major mistake."

Zane knew both of those things were true. The problem was, he couldn't deny how much he wanted *that* to happen again or how *that* hadn't felt like a mistake at all. In fact, it kind of felt like he and Sabrina had just been picking up where they left off the night they were together. As if the last few months never happened, and this was how that night should have ended—in the dawn of a new day, one where they were wrapped in each other's arms. A day the two of them then spent together. Doing the kind of things people did after they'd just had the most spectacular night of their life and wanted to make sure it happened again. And again.

"I am so sorry," Sabrina said.

"I am, too," Zane told her. Even though he kind of wasn't.

"It won't happen again," she added.

He nodded. Then when he remembered her back was to him so she couldn't see it, he told her, "No, it won't."

"Pregnancy hormones," she said. "I've discovered they can do weird things to the brain."

"Right."

"So that's what happened. Pregnancy hormones."

Which maybe explained her actions, but not his. And which meant they had another five or six months of this unless they steered clear of each other. Though that would be a bit difficult when they were going to have to spend so much time together preparing for their babies' births.

There was another long moment of silence, then, very softly, Sabrina said, "We should probably head down to the motel dining room for some breakfast and then make our way back to Chatelaine."

In a matter of minutes, they were seated at a table, but the awkwardness between them showed no sign of abating anytime soon. Remembering his promise of solidarity with Sabrina, Zane opted to eat the same thing for breakfast that Sabrina did—plain Greek yogurt with fruit and a muffin on the side. *Oh, boy. Yummy.* At least there was coffee. Decaf. Yay. But after a few swallows of that, he pretty much managed to fool his brain into thinking it was real coffee and at least felt coherent enough to try to make conversation. Just, you know, not about what had happened that morning.

"We should still be able to beat the delivery truck back to Chatelaine," he told Sabrina. Who was looking at everything in the dining room except him, he couldn't help noticing.

"It's fine if we're not," she said. "I can text Dahlia or Jade and ask if one of them can wait at my house for me. They both live close by enough to be there in minutes."

"And Astrid's at my place," Zane said.

And that was pretty much the extent of his dialogue, at least until he had a couple more cups of fake coffee in him. And even then, he had no idea what to say. He told himself it was because his brain was too smart to fall for the no-it's-really-caffeinated lie. But it was more because the memory of their steamy morning embrace was crowding out every other thought that tried to enter his brain. And every time it did, he got hot and bothered all over again. When he looked at Sabrina, it was to see her still driving her gaze over everything except him. Her cheeks were stained pink, though, and he wondered if maybe she was having as much trouble forgetting about this morning as he was.

And if she was, what were they going to do about it?

"So then I guess we're good," she said.

"I guess we are."

Wow, if this was any example of how their conversation was going to go for the rest of the day, it would be a long, boring drive back to Chatelaine. But maybe that was a good thing. After this morning, they needed boring. Boring was safe. Unremarkable. And led to absolutely nothing. All they had to do now was figure out how to keep things lackluster for the next few months.

He looked at Sabrina. She looked back at him. And just like that, little explosions went off all over his body. Oh, boy. It wasn't just going to be a long drive back to Chatelaine. It was going to be a long five or six months.

Chapter Eight

Sabrina couldn't remember the last time she and her family sat down to have breakfast together. Not since coming to Chatelaine, for sure. So when Wendy invited them all over to her place a few days after Sabrina's tumultuous morning wake-up with Zane, she welcomed the chance to see everyone. Especially her sisters, whom she was hoping to steal away for a bit to share what happened with Zane and ask them if she could keep blaming pregnancy hormones for her increasing attraction to the father of her children. Or if maybe, possibly, there could be something more going on with her and Zane than that.

Her mom had done a lot with the ranch's main house since moving in, making the place feel warm and cozy in spite of its large size. Sabrina and her siblings all knew their mother was still acclimating to living by herself after their father's death. Although Wendy's marriage to Casper had been rocky at times, it had lasted thirty-three years and produced six children. It couldn't be easy to go from a crowded house full of family in the place where you grew up to living in a big mansion alone in a new place. They'd all done their best to drop by for visits or get Wendy out of the house and into Chatelaine proper when they could. But they knew she still felt lonely sometimes. A couple of Sabrina's siblings had even tried setting their mother up with one of the handful of eligible bachelors her age that they'd met since moving to town, but Wendy had shot down all their efforts. It was good, though, to see her gathering her family around her again this way.

"All right," Wendy said when all of her children were seated in the dining room. "I want us to go around the table, and I want to hear what each and every one of you has been up to. Sabrina first."

Dangit. Sabrina knew she should have sat farther away from her mother than immediately to her right. This could be tricky. How did one tell one's mother that one almost had another one-night stand with one's previous one-night stand?

Thankfully, Wendy clarified. "How are my granddaughters doing in there?"

Her mom was over the moon at the prospect of welcoming not just her first, but her second grandchild into the family. She called Sabrina almost daily to chat about how to take care of herself and what to expect when expecting twins, since she'd gone through it twice herself, and no two pregnancies were the same, and, by the way, while they were on the subject, was there any news Sabrina wanted to tell her mother about how she and her baby daddy were getting along?

"You mean since we spoke on the phone yesterday?" Sabrina asked with a smile. "I imagine they've gained a couple millimeters or two in length and probably at least a tenth of an ounce in weight."

Her mother made a face at her. "Oh, you. Have you felt the twins moving around yet?"

Sabrina shook her head wistfully. "Not yet. Soon I hope."

Wendy directed her attention to her youngest son, on Sabrina's other side. "And, Ridge, how are Hope and Evie doing?"

"As well as can be expected," he replied. "She's still having those dreams about the older couple, and their faces are a little less cloudy than they were at first, but she still doesn't recognize them or even know if they're real people or just, you know, dreams."

One by one, Wendy went around the table asking her children how everything was going in their respective lives, and one by one, they all told her. Sabrina learned that Jade's high school reunion was coming up next month, that Nash was genuinely enjoying being foreman of the Fortune ranch, that her brother Arlo was thinking about investing in yet another ranch he wanted to turn around and that Dahlia's herd of sheep was coming along nicely. Which, oh, goody, meant more wool for Sabrina to use at her textile camp—provided Dahlia could spare any this early in her venture—once Zane finally realized that revitalizing his own pond was a much better option for his ranch than trying to steal land she already owned.

The family had finished breakfast, and Sabrina and her siblings were cleaning up the aftermath when, out of nowhere, the sound of cell phone notifications from pockets and purses interrupted their animated conversations.

"Must be one of those county-wide alerts about something," Arlo said, pulling his own phone from his back pocket. His expression changed, though, when he read what was on the screen. "What the heck? Not this again."

The other Fortunes all pulled out their own phones to see what their notifications were about since, presumably, they all received the same one.

"It's from the mystery wedding person again," Dahlia said.

A month ago, all the Fortunes, Wendy and her children alike, had received save-the-date cards for a wedding to take place in January. There was just one problem—none of them knew who had sent the invitations, and none of them knew anyone who was planning on getting married, in January or any other month. Especially anyone in Chatelaine, which was where the wedding would be taking place. Now all of them were receiving a text from an unidentified number Sabrina could only assume was the same person who sent the invites.

"Anybody have this number in their contacts list?" she asked them all. "'Cause it's sure not in mine."

All of her siblings and her mother said no.

"But it must be the same person who sent us the save-the-dates, right?" Jade asked.

It was safe to assume that, yes. But it didn't make the text any less baffling.

Dear Wedding Guests, it read. Which dress and suit do you like best? A, B or C? What followed was a string of photographs of different styles of wedding garb varying from western to formal to what Sabrina could only liken to "down home."

"It was weird when we got the invites last month," Ridge said, "and it's even weirder getting texts now."

"Right?" Jade agreed. "Whoever is doing this must know us all. Who could it be?"

"Obviously someone who has all our numbers," Arlo said.

"So who has all our numbers?" Dahlia asked.

The family members all exchanged curious looks. None had an answer.

"It must be someone from Cactus Grove," Sabrina said. "We haven't been in Chatelaine long enough for someone to have collected *all* our numbers."

"Unless Mom's been handing them out," Dahlia said with a meaningful look at their mother.

Wendy held up her hands in mock surrender. "Don't look at me. I never give out your all's contact information without asking your permission first."

Which Sabrina figured was true. Her mother was an absolute tigress when it came to protecting her children.

"Wonder who else they texted?" Jade asked.

"Looks like just the seven of us," Nash replied after a tap on his phone. "Unless they blind cc'ed a bunch of other people. But I'm not sure how you'd do that without making the text an SMS, and this one doesn't appear to be that."

"Let's take another approach," Dahlia said. "Who do we know that likes dresses like these?" She scrolled through each of the photos on her phone, back and forth and back again.

"Or who do we know who likes suits like these?" Arlo added, doing the same kind of scrolling himself.

"Ask me," Ridge said, "I wouldn't be caught dead in the monkey suit."

"Yeah," Nash agreed. "I hate having to put on one of those things when I have to go to some big to-do."

"Besides, Nash is more of the square-dancing type," Arlo quipped, holding up the western-wear photo.

"That's not what men wear to square dance," Wendy chastened. "I actually kind of like that one. I like the tuxedo, too, though. And the last one."

"I like C best," Ridge said. "Only not in that awful pale blue."

"I like the blue," Wendy objected.

"Mom's just being polite," Ridge said. "In case the sender works for the NSA and is listening in on our conversation. Blind ccs and all that."

Wendy playfully swatted her youngest, and they all laughed. "I just can't decide which one I like best is all."

"I like C best, too," Sabrina said, agreeing with her youngest brother. "The dress especially."

"You don't think it's too plain?" Dahlia asked.

"It's perfect," Jade agreed. "I can see Dolly Parton in the first one, though, so there's that. Dolly can do no wrong."

"B is too formal, though," Dahlia said. "Pretty, but too conventional. People should do their own thing for their weddings and not succumb to tradition."

"Spoken like someone who married on the fly in Vegas," Sabrina said with a grin. She still couldn't quite stop needling her sister about the circumstances of her wedding, since it sounded like something from a rom-com.

This time it was Dahlia who did the swatting.

"Stop!" Sabrina said, laughing.

Dahlia gave her twin one last thwack, then she laughed, too.

"Maybe it is the NSA," Ridge said, laughing along with his sisters. "It would explain how they got all our numbers."

"I guess we'll solve the mystery of who this is from at the wedding in January," Dahlia said, "and which outfits they end up choosing."

"But why is it such a big mystery?" Sabrina wondered aloud. "Usually people can't wait to tell everyone they're getting married."

"We'll just have to wait for an actual invitation," Jade said. "First one who gets one, let the rest of us know."

It was with no small amount of trepidation that Sabrina pulled her car to a stop in front of Zane's house the Friday following the weird wedding text breakfast with her family. She didn't know why she was so nervous. It was only dinner. Okay, admittedly *with his entire big family*, whom she had yet to meet, but still just a meal. He was going to be dining with her and her entire big family at her place next week, too, so that all of Peach's and Plum's clans on both their parents' sides could get to know each other before their arrival. Co-parenting meant co-familying, too, she and Zane had decided.

The minute she opened her car door, she heard sounds of raucous joy coming from inside the house. It was a beautiful, balmy evening, so the windows were open wide, and the large great room, she recalled, faced the front. When she looked in that direction, she could see bodies darting about and hear music playing, something twangy and folksy and fun. She inhaled a deep breath, reminded herself that everything was going to be just fine, then began to make her way toward the front door.

Astrid was opening it before Sabrina even made it to the porch, the housekeeper's smile warm and welcoming. "Miss Fortune," she said. "It is so nice to see you again."

"Please call me Sabrina, Astrid," she replied. "Something tells me we're going to be seeing a lot of each other before too long."

"I look forward to that, Miss Fortune," Astrid said. "It will be nice to have the sound of children's laughter in the house."

Okay, they could work on the *Miss Fortune* thing later, Sabrina thought as she made her way into the house proper.

The festivity grew louder as she walked deeper inside. And when she arrived at the great room, it was to discover there were even more people present than just Zane and his brothers, including some young women who were clearly *not* brothers, presumably girlfriends of some of the boys. Everyone seemed to notice her entrance at once, because they all stopped talking and looked her way. Not even in those anxiety dreams about being naked in public had Sabrina felt more on display.

She glanced down to make sure she had in fact re-

membered to put on clothes before she left. Yep, she'd
even correctly buttoned her lavender, untucked blouse—
the one that hid the unfastened fly of her jeans—and she
had her flat gold sandals on the right feet. Okay, maybe
she hadn't done the best job with her braid, but the es-
caped tendrils she could feel framing her face were
fashionable. She was almost sure of it. Then she looked
back up at the crowd. They all broke out in smiles and
laughter again, and ran over to make her acquaintance.

"All right, all right, don't overwhelm her," Zane said
as his family descended. "You don't want to scare her
off before she's even learned which one of you is which."

With clear reluctance, the crowd of young people
reined themselves in. Barely. Zane looked gorgeous, as
always, tonight wearing dark jeans and a plaid western
shirt in every color of green that made his eyes even
brighter than usual. He'd gotten a haircut in the days
since she'd seen him, something she had mixed feelings
about. On one hand, the shorter style also showcased
his eyes and chiseled features. On the other, she kind
of liked him rakishly scruffy-looking.

He gazed at her nervously for a minute, as if he
wasn't sure how to greet her. Then, softly, he said, "Hey,
thanks for coming," leaned in to give her a quick kiss
on the cheek, then settled his arm loosely around her
waist. There was nothing untoward in either gesture.
Both were clearly light and affectionate. Before she realized what she was doing, Sabrina was leaning into him,
too, and wrapping her arm around his waist as well.

And wow, there went the spine-sizzling heat again,
just with those two simple gestures. She was beginning

to wonder if there would ever come a time when she didn't feel hot and bothered around Zane.

She pushed the thought away, smiled as amiably as she could and lifted her other hand in greeting. "Hello," she said to the room at large. "I'm Sabrina."

The boys all began to talk at once, so Zane lifted his hand to stop them. "I'll make the introductions," he said over all their voices, loudly enough—and with enough big brother authority—that they all piped down.

He pointed at the brother standing closest to him and said, "This is Cody, my youngest. And mouthiest," he added with a grin.

"Hey, I'm not the mouthiest," Cody objected playfully. "I'm the most verbally gifted."

The others howled at that.

"And this is his girlfriend, Hannah." Zane indicated the cute, petite redhead beside him.

Although he'd introduced both kids warmly, there was something in his voice that made her think his relationship with them at the moment was a tad cool. Then she remembered how, the day she'd come here to tell him about her pregnancy, Zane mentioned having to talk Cody out of running away to join the rodeo with his girlfriend. He was probably still worried about the possibility. Then again, when she and Preston had been their age, they'd been chomping at the bit to get out from under their parents' thumbs and live their own life together, too. Zane might very well have a reason to be concerned.

"This is Wyatt, my oldest younger brother," Zane continued, gesturing toward the next boy in line. "And his girlfriend Lakshmi," he added for the dark-haired, dark-eyed girl beside him.

Wyatt extended a hand in an assertive, *I'm-the-oldest-brother-okay-except-for-Zane* fashion, and Sabrina shook it. "Really glad you could come tonight, Sabrina," he said. "We've all been looking forward to meeting you."

The others murmured their agreement and, Sabrina couldn't help noticing, seemed to be steering their gazes to her abdomen, where their future nieces were currently residing. She did her best not to chuckle.

"This is Shane, one of the twins," Zane continued down the line. "And his boyfriend Esteban."

Shane nodded and Esteban smiled as both said their hellos to her.

"And this is Levi, the other twin," Zane said as he gestured at the last boy in the group.

"No, Shane is the other twin," Levi countered. "I came first. He's the backup."

Sabrina laughed at that. She was going to have to use it on Dahlia at some point, since Dahlia was a whole twenty-two minutes younger than her.

"My girlfriend, Chloe, couldn't make it," Levi continued. "She's doing a study-abroad in Japan this semester. But she'll be back by Christmas vacation, so you can meet her then."

Sabrina would be seven months pregnant at Christmastime. Peach and Plum would probably be more like Pumpkin and Watermelon by then. And Sabrina would be as big as the Alamo. Oh, boy. She couldn't wait.

She marveled at Zane's family. They all seemed so… young. She found herself wondering what her daughters would be like as teenagers and college students, then stopped herself. *Don't wish it away*, she cautioned herself. Once those girls were born, time, she was certain, would zip by faster than the speed of light.

"It's nice to meet all of you," she told them. "And have faces to put to names for the girls' uncles."

She almost added *and aunts, too*, but didn't want to presume. They all were really young, and people did come and go in life. Then she glanced at Cody and Hannah, at the way they were gazing at each other. Oh, that was a familiar look, she couldn't help thinking. She used to look at Preston like that. Young love was a powerful force. Something told her that *Aunt Hannah* would indeed eventually be a part of the girls' lives.

Then she looked at Zane and wondered how she looked at him lately. What she'd felt for her husband way back when had been so immediate, so intense. The way feelings so often were when one was a teenager. What she felt for Zane, though… Well, certainly there had been an immediacy and intensity between them when they met. Doubtless because he'd made her feel like a teenager that night. Since seeing him again, though, things had felt a lot less… Well. Her feelings were deeper and more complicated than the lightheartedness and lightheadedness that came with youth. What she was feeling for him was fuller somehow. More dimensional. More adult. More everything, really. She just wished she knew what to do about it.

"Come on," he told the group. "Astrid said dinner would be served at seven sharp, and you know how she is."

Shane looked at his watch as he took Esteban's hand. "We only have thirty seconds," he told his companions. "We better hurry."

Zane reached for Sabrina's hand, too, and she twined her fingers with his as if it were the most natural thing in the world to do. And somehow, she knew that feeling wasn't entirely due to the fact that the two of them would be co-parenting their daughters.

Dinner was, not surprisingly, delicious. Who knew a Valkyrie who made havreflarns and cloudberry tea could also create the best chicken enchilada casserole and jalapeño corn bread Sabrina had ever tasted? One thing she didn't have to worry about where the twins were concerned was whether or not they'd be properly fed during the time they spent at their father's place. Sabrina only wondered if maybe she could stay over with them sometimes.

There it was again. A stray wish to take up residence here at Zane's ranch. Just what was her brain trying to tell her these days?

The dinner conversation was all over the map, with Zane's family talking about everything from childhood vacations to family pets to failed school projects. Eventually, though, the discussion veered to focus on Zane. Including, inescapably, Zane's former girlfriends.

"So, Sabrina," Wyatt said over the remnants of dessert, "did Zane ever tell you about the girlfriend he had who quoted poetry every time she talked?"

The other brothers laughed.

"And not even her own poetry," Wyatt added. "It was all stuff from hundreds of years ago."

"Including *The Canterbury Tales*," Shane said. "In Middle English."

"It was when I was in college," Zane told Sabrina. "She was an English major. A really serious one."

Sabrina chuckled. College years really could be blunder years.

"Or the one who got busted for growing weed and mushrooms on the campus quad," Levi added, "and then tried to pass them off as requirements for one of her labs."

"Also college," Zane assured her. "She was a biology major."

"Oh, don't forget when he used the dating app!" Cody added.

"No," Zane said decisively. "We are not going to talk about the dating app. I was only on it for two weeks."

His brothers all snickered.

"And in two weeks," Shane said, "you had, what? Five first dates that ended really badly?"

"Or didn't even get started," Levi stated. "There was the woman who, as soon as the server brought the bread basket, starting tearing it up and putting it in her purse to feed her pet rat that she'd brought along."

"Which was a health code violation," Zane said. "So I had every right to leave after prepaying the bill."

"And the one who, halfway through dinner," Cody added, "whipped out her multilevel marketing campaign and gave a thirty-minute spiel loud enough to lasso in the whole restaurant."

Zane laughed a little anxiously and threw Sabrina a

nervous look. "Well, at least it was for a product that could have some potential use."

"Oh, I'm sure lots of people at Chez Whatever It Was were chomping at the bit to buy sex toys that night."

Sabrina wished she could laugh along with the rest of his family, but she wasn't finding all the talk of Zane's past, ah, *romantic encounters*, particularly funny. And not just because they were clearly making him uncomfortable, too.

"And don't forget the Elvis impersonator!" Wyatt added with a laugh.

Zane seemed to sense her apprehension, because he lifted a hand and told his brothers to knock it off. "That app stuff was years ago," he added. "And all it ended up doing was cementing my conviction that romantic love doesn't exist."

Sabrina told herself she should be happy to hear him say that, since she no longer believed romantic love existed, either. For some reason, though, his assertion was accompanied by a sick feeling in the pit of her stomach.

Indigestion, she told herself. She'd started having episodes of that as her pregnancy moved along. What she was feeling had nothing to do with anything Zane said. She'd just overdone it on the enchilada casserole.

But the brothers weren't quite ready to let their roasting of their big brother go and went on to describe a litany of other less-than-stellar experiences Zane had had with women over the years, going all the way back to high school. And even if none of those encounters had been particularly, ah, productive, they kind of flew in the face of his assurances to Sabrina that he hadn't been involved with very many women. No, maybe he hadn't been in many serious relationships, but he certainly had more experience with the opposite sex than Sabrina did. And why that bothered her, she had no idea. It just kind of skirted dishonesty on his part somehow. She found herself wondering if there were other things he hadn't exactly been honest about, either.

"Wow, Zane," she said when the levity was dying down. She tried to inject a lightness into her voice that she was nowhere close to feeling as she added, "You've dated a lot more women than you let on."

"No. I haven't," he tried to reassure her. He shot his brothers a good, long glare. "These guys are exaggerating. Hard."

But she couldn't help noticing he hadn't said they weren't telling the truth.

"Okay, I have *dated* my fair share of women," he said, backpedaling. "But dating didn't mean I was involved with any of them."

"This is true," Levi said when he seemed to realize Sabrina was taking their ribbing of Zane way more seriously than they intended. "He never brought any of those women home to meet us. We only know about them because they came up during the talk about red flags when we were all old enough to start dating."

The other brothers all nodded earnestly.

She wished she could believe that. But after an evening filled with so many, ah, revelations, not all of which had been exactly good, it wasn't doing much to help the nausea rolling in her stomach. She did her best to smile one of her no-hard-feelings smiles in an effort to pretend it didn't matter. Fortunately, she must have been at least a little convincing, because the conversation started up again, this time with much better stories about Zane.

How he let Wyatt beat him at chess when he was teaching him how to play.

How patient he was with Cody when he couldn't figure out a ring knot.

How he came to every opening night Levi had in drama club and sat front row, center stage, even when the play was the student-written *FOMO and Juul-iet*, which, yes, he admitted was every bit as terrible as it sounded.

And finally, how accepting and loving he was when Shane was terrified to come out and tell his big, brash cattleman brother he was gay.

That was when Sabrina realized maybe she was being too hard on Zane and that, yes, he was as good a guy as she had realized from the moment they met. This house really did feel a lot different when it was full of his family than it had when she was here visiting him alone. She understood now why he had been so happy when she told him she was pregnant. Houses like this had been built at a time and in a place where families were big and rowdy and boisterous. Just like Zane's. He really was going to be a wonderful father, she thought, regardless of how they worked out the co-parenting thing.

Which they *were* going to work out. Any day now.

Chapter Nine

Zane and Cody had just started rinsing the dishes to put in the dishwasher when he realized his brother hadn't said a word since dinner. Which was funny, considering he'd been the most vociferous of all of them when it came to razzing his big brother earlier. It was the main reason, actually, that he'd asked his youngest sibling to help him clean up instead of one of the older boys. He'd felt more comfortable leaving Sabrina to get to know the rest of his family because the rabble-rouser was in here with him instead. The other boys had matured quite a bit since heading off to college, but Cody still had a lot of growing up to do. It was just another reason he was adamant that the kid get his degree. And on that note…

"So how's school been since our last talk?" he asked matter-of-factly. "Settling in a little better?"

Cody didn't answer at first. He seemed way more concerned about making sure the glassware was lined up on the top rack with perfect precision. Zane noted a movement at the kitchen door behind his brother and saw Sabrina, who was carrying a stray plate they must have left behind. She seemed to sense the stilted mood in the kitchen, however, because the smile on her face fell, and she closed her mouth over whatever she had planned to say. Zane threw her a grateful look but didn't indicate she should leave. In fact, he was kind of glad to have her here, even if it was just for moral support. Not to mention she just looked really pretty this evening.

Cody hadn't noticed her arrival. When he finally looked up at Zane, it was with an expression of consternation. "It sucks," he grumbled. "I hate it. I don't want to go to college, Zane. I wanna rodeo."

Instead of jumping down his brother's throat about that—*again*—Zane tried to be understanding. "I know you do. But you have plenty of time for that, and college—"

"College won't teach me anything I need to know," Cody interrupted. "It'll just waste time. Time I could be using honing my skills. I'm a good cowboy," he insisted when Zane tried to interrupt. "And Hannah blue-ribboned in three events at the Barrel Blast last summer. She and I are both ready for rodeo *now*."

Helplessly, Zane looked at Sabrina. She smiled her encouragement but said nothing. This was clearly between him and Cody.

"It's not that easy, Cody," Zane said.

"Yes, it is," his brother countered.

"You're too young. Both of you are. You have no idea what the world out there holds. In a few years, you'll both be in a better position to figure out what you want. What's really important."

Cody growled a sound of frustration. "We already know what we want, Zane!" he shouted. "We know what's important! You're the one who refuses to see it!"

"Cody, you're too young to realize how—"

"I'm eighteen!"

"Exactly."

"I'm old enough to vote, to be sent to war, to serve on a jury, to get a credit card, to buy a house… I can do damn near anything I want to."

Zane hated that he couldn't argue with any of that. Even so, Cody was still too young to be making big decisions.

"And you know what else I can do now that I'm eighteen?" he asked, his voice filled with challenge. "I can refuse to go to college. I can get married to the woman I love. And you know what, Zane? Hannah and I might just do that. We don't need your permission. We don't even have to tell you about it. We can just run off and elope. And then join the rodeo. With or without your consent."

As if to illustrate that that was exactly what he and Hannah were going to do, Cody jutted up his chin, guided the upper rack into the dishwasher and closed the door. Then, very calmly, he turned to walk out of the kitchen. He paused when he saw Sabrina, but only for a second. Then he strode right past her.

As he did, he said, "See if you can talk some sense into him, Sabrina. Tell him I'm right."

And then he was gone, back out to join his brothers. And his would-be fiancée. A bolt of something hot and unpleasant shot through Zane's brain at the very idea of him and Hannah running off to get married and his not being able to do a thing to stop it.

"Do you believe that?" he said after his brother was gone.

"Which part?" Sabrina asked. "About him not wanting to go to college? Yes, I believe that. College isn't for everyone."

"It is for my family. Like I told you before, my parents set up college funds for all of us. They were adamant that we all get degrees. Didn't matter what in. Just that we got a college education. If they were in this kitchen right now and heard what Cody just said, they'd be telling him the same thing I did."

And they would have. Of that, Zane was absolutely certain.

"That doesn't necessarily mean they'd be right," Sabrina told him softly. "And really, Cody wasn't wrong about the other stuff, either."

She might as well have just smacked him across the face with a wet fish. "How do you figure that?"

"Eighteen is the legal age to do all the things he mentioned," she said. "Plus a million more. The US government thinks it's perfectly okay to let Cody make big decisions at his age. A lot of eighteen-year-olds have taken on way more responsibility than Cody has, and they're doing just fine."

"A lot of kids his age aren't my little brother."

"No, they're not," she agreed. "But you're not your little brother, either, Zane."

Ouch.

She took a few more steps into the kitchen and set the stray plate in the sink with the others he and Cody hadn't finished loading. Then she turned to look at him full on. Only inches separated them now, and he realized he'd done her wrong by saying she only looked pretty tonight. Truth was, Sabrina was the most beautiful woman he'd ever seen. Her lavender shirt somehow made her eyes look bluer, and her pale blond bangs were wisps of silk falling over her forehead. She smelled nice, too, something floral and spicy and downright irresistible. It was all he could do not to lean in for more.

"I wasn't much older than Cody when I married Preston," she said. "But we might as well have married when we were eighteen. Both of us knew we were ready. And yes, maybe it didn't turn out so well for us, but that had nothing to do with our maturity level."

He sobered at that. Okay, yeah. Maybe there were a lot of young people out there who learned hard lessons earlier than other people did. Sabrina had learned one of the worst after losing her husband when she was so young.

"We knew our parents would react the same way you're reacting to Cody right now," she went on, "and even if they'd forbidden us to get married, we would have done it, anyway. We would have turned our backs on both our families and gone our own way without them. Is that what you want to have happen to Cody? To forbid him from following his heart and losing him?"

"Of course not. But he's—"

"He's going to do what he wants to do, Zane. You telling him he can't is just going to make him more determined. And if you keep it up, it's just going to ensure that he never speaks to you again."

Zane felt so helpless. He'd spent the last ten years being the final word for all four of his brothers. The older ones had always heeded his decisions. But then, they'd all agreed with those decisions. They'd all wanted to go to college. But Cody had always been such a handful. So high-spirited and willful. So…so…

"He is so young, Sabrina," Zane said quietly. "He has no idea what the real world is like."

"Maybe. Maybe not. He might know a lot more than you think. But that's just it, Zane. It's up to him to find out. It's not up to you to protect him for the rest of his life."

She was right. He knew she was right. But that didn't make it any easier for him to accept. Still, maybe he and Cody needed to sit down and have a longer talk about what he really wanted, and what all that involved. More to the point, maybe Zane should listen to his little brother. Then maybe they could find some kind of common ground.

Maybe.

"Is this the way you're gonna be with Peach and Plum?" he asked Sabrina.

She laughed and relaxed a little. She untangled the arms she'd crossed as she'd spoken about her marriage, settling one on the kitchen counter and the other on her hip. "Probably not," she admitted. "I'll probably be as fierce a protector of them as you are of your brothers. But I hope that at least part of me will be able to see that they're their own person and that it's only up to me to do my best to educate and guide them and hope they make good decisions once they're on their own."

"And if they don't make good decisions?"

She lifted one shoulder and let it drop. Then she raised the hand on her hip to cup his cheek gently in her palm. Warmth spread from Zane's face to every other part of his body at the contact.

"Then I'll be there to catch them when they fall," she said softly. "Just like you will be."

Zane covered her hand with his and smiled. Then he removed it and pressed her palm to his lips, giving it a quick kiss before moving both their hands back between them. But he didn't let go.

"I guess that's really what parenting comes down to in the long run, isn't it?" he said. "Being there for your kids not just when they succeed, but when they fail, too."

She nodded. "Probably something you and I should do for each other, too," she said. "Have each other's backs, I mean."

He gave her fingers a gentle squeeze then, reluctantly, let her hand go. "This isn't going to be easy, is it?" he asked. "This parenting stuff."

Sabrina sighed. "I'm guessing no. But I'm also guessing it will have rewards that make up for that."

Zane nodded. Not sure anything else needed to be said on that score, he turned his attention to the still-not-cleaned-up kitchen and shook his head. "Hopefully there will also be rewards when they stiff you on the cleanups they promised they'd help with."

She chuckled. "Let him visit with his brothers and girlfriend. They're only home for the weekend. I'll help you clean up."

Zane nodded. "Thanks. Probably best to leave Cody be for now, anyway. Pushing him any more could just make things worse."

"And I need to get used to cleaning up after more than just me," she said as she joined him at the sink.

He laughed, too. "Oh, cleaning up after the Baston bunch will definitely help you out on that score."

Cleaning up after a large family was more time-consuming than Sabrina would have guessed. In fact, by the time she and Zane returned to the dining room to rejoin his family and their various significant others, every last one of them had disappeared.

"Okay, that wasn't exactly a quick cleanup," she said, "but it's way too early for any of them to have turned in for the night."

Zane seemed just as puzzled. He looked as if he was going to reply when his gaze lit on something at the center of the table. She watched as he approached, then picked up a pad of paper, holding it up for her to see that there was a note scrawled on it. For a minute, she feared maybe Cody and Hannah really had run off to elope, taking the rest of the dinner guests with them as witnesses. But judging by the smile on Zane's face as he read over the missive, that wasn't the case at all.

"They've all gone into Chatelaine for trivia night at Remi's Reads," he said when he looked up. "Remi's does it every few months. It's a pretty big deal. Chatelaine Bar and Grill donates pizza. The LC Club donates a grand prize of dinner for two. There's gift cards and other stuff from some of the other restaurants." He nodded toward the note again. "My brothers also say they're all going to grab a bite to eat afterward. Guess enchilada casserole and dessert, not to mention free pizza, just isn't enough when you're a growing boy or girl. And they say that they're doing all this so that us *lovebirds*—" he pointed at the note "—their word, not mine, can have some time alone. You and I have been directed to go to the library."

Sabrina grinned. "And what are we supposed to find there?"

"No telling. Probably should check it out, though, to make sure it's nothing that needs care or feeding. Wouldn't be the first time one of those boys smuggled in a stray something or other and stayed mum until it was too late for me to do anything about it. That's how we wound up with six barn cats at one point."

"Then by all means, lead the way."

The library was upstairs and down the hall from Zane's office, Sabrina discovered, and it was just as rustic and masculine as the rest of the house. There was a fireplace, though, where someone—gosh, no telling who—had lit a small, cozy fire. Someone else had placed an ice bucket holding a bottle of something with two slender flutes before it, and a cozy-looking throw had been spread out like a picnic blanket. And yet another someone had set up the sound system to play music that was soft and sexy and full of saxophones.

"Gee, this isn't obvious at all, is it?" Zane said in a deadpan voice.

"This is exactly what a college student would consider a romantic scenario," Sabrina replied. "It's straight out of Hollywood."

Of course, it wasn't just college students and Hollywood who would think that. She thought it was pretty romantic, too. Shame about the wine, though.

As if reading her mind, Zane crossed to the ice bucket to withdraw the bottle from the ice. Then he smiled again. "Sparkling apple juice," he said. He squinted at some numbers around the neck. "Bottled this year, no less. An excellent vintage, even if it is a screw top."

"Best not let it go to waste then," Sabrina agreed.

She joined him at the fireplace, and he poured each of them a glass. Then he looked around the room again. "Hmm. That sofa over there—" he gestured to a love seat that had been awkwardly shoved to one side "—is supposed to be right here in front of the fireplace where people can sit to enjoy it. Looks like someone—" no telling who "—decided to do some rearranging."

"The blanket is fine," Sabrina told him.

"You sure?"

She nodded. "It will be good to stretch out my legs."

He set their glasses on the hearth, then folded himself, legs crossed pretzel fashion, onto the blanket. Then he held up his hand toward Sabrina, who took it and managed to situate herself beside him. She realized pretty quickly, though, that yes, she could indeed stretch out her legs, but she had nothing to lean against as she did. Zane seemed to realize her dilemma, because he moved closer and positioned himself so that she could lean back against him. Then, just to be sure she didn't tip over, he put his arm around her. She gratefully leaned into him, accepted the glass of juice he held out to her and listened to the soft crackle of the fire. And she tried very, very hard not to think about how good she felt in that moment.

Pregnancy hormones, she tried to tell herself again. But, really, she was beginning not to believe herself when she said that. She hadn't been pregnant when she met Zane that night at the fundraiser. And the way she was feeling right now was a lot like the way she'd felt that night.

For a few minutes, neither seemed to know what to say. Then Zane asked, "So…how have you been feeling lately? Good?"

She nodded. "The nausea I was feeling before I saw the doctor has pretty much gone away. I get tired a lot, though. Sometimes so tired that I have to lie down for a little while or even take a nap. But the doctor said that's normal. Good, actually, because it means the babies are growing well."

"Have you felt them move yet?"

She shook her head. "Still too soon according to the reading I've been doing. But I'm hopeful it won't be too long. Especially since there are two of them in there."

"You'll tell me when that happens, right?"

She turned her head to look at him. How could he think she would keep that from him? "You'll know the second I do."

He smiled. "Thanks."

Due to their position on the floor, their faces were so close. Mere inches separated Zane's mouth from hers. His eyes, those gorgeous green eyes she'd nearly drowned in the night she met him, were clear and bright and happy, and she felt herself going deep under, the same way she had then.

"So," she said in an effort to keep herself from succumbing, "it was nice of Astrid to stay late tonight to fix dinner."

She told herself to move away, to figure out how to be comfortable without the toasty warm feeling of having Zane beside her, because just changing the subject did nothing to keep her from melting into this man.

"She was happy to do it," he said softly. "She misses the boys, too, and loves to be around when they're home. I think she's going to be hovering over Peach and Plum, too, whenever they come to visit. I saw some booties-in-progress in her knitting basket the other day. She never had kids herself, so she's getting her Amma on with the twins."

"Amma?" Sabrina asked, still way more focused on Zane's amazing eyes—they had a tiny circle of gold around the pupil that was mesmerizing—than what they were talking about. What were they talking about, anyway?

"That's a Viking word for grandmother," Zane said, the words tumbling into her ears on a warm breath. "Or so Astrid said. In a not-so-subtle hint."

Sabrina smiled. "My mother is still trying to decide what she wants her grandbabies to call her. Though last time we talked, she was leaning toward Glamma."

He chuckled lightly.

"That or Queenie."

Now he laughed outright. "I wish my folks could be around to meet their granddaughters. Your mom would have to fight my mom for Queenie."

"Your folks will be around, Zane," she said with quiet

certainty. "Every time you look at your daughters, your mom and dad both will be right there."

For another long moment, neither said a word. Then, very slowly, Zane started to lower his head toward hers. Without even thinking about what she was doing, Sabrina tipped her head back, too. Then he was covering her mouth with his, brushing his lips lightly over hers, sending heat splashing through her belly and to all points beyond. When he pulled away, she curled her hand around his nape and pulled him back. This time she was the one to kiss him, in the same sweet, gentle way he had her.

Then the song that had been playing so quietly in the background segued into another, and both Zane and Sabrina smiled.

"You remember this song?" he asked.

She nodded. "Oh, yes. This is the song we danced to that night at the fundraiser."

"And if memory serves, we didn't get to finish it."

They hadn't, actually. Because Zane had danced her out of the hotel ballroom and into the fair, fine night outside, across the patio and onto the hotel grounds, all the way to the secluded gazebo where they shared their first kiss. And then their second. And their third. And there probably would have been a fourth, fifth and sixth if Zane hadn't asked her if she wanted to blow off the rest of the fundraiser and go home with him instead. And, of course, if Sabrina hadn't eagerly said yes.

He brushed his lips over hers once more. "So you wanna finish it now?"

She grinned. "I'd love to."

He stood and extended a hand toward her, pulling her up alongside him after she accepted it. Then he roped an arm around her waist and took her hand in his. She'd forgotten what a good dancer he was and remembered how she'd wanted to ask him where he learned that night of the fundraiser, before the two of them got sidetracked.

So she asked him now, "Where did you learn to dance?"

He chuckled and groaned at the same time. "My mother made me take cotillion classes when I was in middle school," he told her. "She was so sure they'd come in handy when I started dating, and then I'd be all set for my wedding day."

She tried to imagine an adolescent Zane in a ballroom full of other kids, all of them awkward and uncertain. But she couldn't. She'd bet he was every bit as confident and suave as he was now. Every girl in his class had probably wanted him for her partner.

"I hated it," he told her. "But believe it or not, I honestly think it made me a better rider. Gave me better balance in the saddle. I made all the boys do cotillion, too. Told them it was what Mom would have wanted. And she would have. If Cody does well in rodeo, he can thank me for making him go to those lessons."

Sabrina smiled inwardly that Zane already seemed to be coming around to his little brother wanting to buck the Baston trend of college. It showed how much he'd listened to Cody tonight. That was a good quality in a parent-to-be.

It was a good quality in a partner, too, she thought before she could stop herself.

ELIZABETH BEVARLY

"Where did you learn to dance?" he asked Sabrina.

By now, he'd guided her all the way around the library and was starting another circle. "Believe it or not, as a college PE credit. They only offered ballroom dancing for one semester because so few students enrolled, but I jumped on it. I was terrible at every sport you can name, but I always loved dancing."

"Well, hopefully our daughters will get your grace and my athleticism."

Our daughters. She was pretty sure that was the first time either of them had said those words out loud in that way. Until now, it had always been *the twins* or *the babies,* or *my twins* or *my babies,* or the nicknames Peach and Plum. She didn't think they'd ever even said *our* twins or *our* babies. But now Zane had said *our daughters* as if it were the most natural thing in the world.

Their gazes connected, as if he had just realizd the same thing, and they were suddenly clicking…or something… in a way they hadn't until now. A way that was more familiar. More intimate. And somehow, in that moment, Sabrina knew they weren't going to finish this dance tonight, either.

As if reading her mind, when Zane danced her toward the library entrance this time, he kept going out into the hall. And then farther, past a half dozen rooms, until he arrived at the one she remembered as being his. He guided her through the door, nudging it closed behind him, and kissed her again. The way he had that night at the fundraiser, in the gazebo. A kiss that had made heat seep into every cell of her body and ignite flames everywhere he touched her.

It had the same effect tonight. But there was more tonight, too. Tonight, his kiss made her feel as if nothing
in her life would ever go wrong again. As if she were
exactly where she was supposed to be in the world. Deep
down in her heart it felt as if the two of them had been
leading up to this moment from the second they met and
were just finishing something they started months ago.

Oh, yes, Sabrina thought when he pulled away to
gaze into her eyes. Everything was just as it was supposed to be.

She wanted Zane. The way she'd had him that night
at the fundraiser, stretched out beside her, nestled on
top of her, moving behind her. She wanted his hands
stroking every inch of her body, wanted to touch every
part of his in return. He seemed to want that, too, because he cupped a hand over her nape and bent his head
to hers again, covering her mouth with his.

He moved his hand from her back to her front, to
free the first few buttons on her shirt. So Sabrina freed
a few of his, too. The silky skin she found underneath
was roped with muscle and sinew and grew hotter everywhere her fingers fell. As she touched him with one
hand, she lifted her other to thread her fingers through
his silky, brown hair, cupping the back of his head to
pull him closer still. She returned his kisses with equal
ardor, and with each brush of her lips over his, her de-
sire for him—her need for him—grew stronger.

He just felt so good. All of him felt so good. He surrounded her somehow, and everything else faded to
nothing. In that moment, Zane was everything. He filled
every corner of her brain, every chamber of her heart,

every breath of her spirit. The thought of that should have overwhelmed her. Somehow, though, it just seemed to fit so perfectly.

When he pulled his mouth from hers, she reluctantly let him go. He didn't go far, though. His face hovered just over hers, his green eyes seeming darker somehow, his lips curved into a tempting little smile.

"Are you sure about this?" he murmured as he lifted a hand to wrap an errant wisp of her hair around his finger.

She nodded. "More than sure. It feels like this has been a long time coming. Like we've wasted so much time tiptoeing around it."

"It does kind of feel like the natural order of things, doesn't it? Like that night four months ago was just a prelude to all this. You and me, right here, right now."

He was right. It felt like no time at all had passed since they'd last been in this room together. Like this was her second chance with him. Her chance to get it right. To wake up beside Zane in the morning instead of escaping under cover of darkness. She smiled. All roads led to Chatelaine. She didn't know why it had taken her so long to see that.

Zane released the strand of hair he'd twisted around his finger and kissed her again, reaching around to free the tie that held what little of her braid that remained in place. He pulled back as the pale blond tresses tumbled free around her shoulders, then buried his fist under the silky mass to curl his fingers around her nape and pull her forward. Nuzzling her throat, he dragged his open mouth lightly up and down the side of her neck, nosing aside the collar of her shirt to kiss her collarbone, too.

As he did, he freed a few more buttons on her shirt and tucked his hand inside, discovering the champagne-colored lace of her bra. He grazed his thumb along the lower line of the garment, skimming his fingers over her sensitive flesh and then lower, over each elegant rib he found. Little bonfires erupted everywhere he touched her. What he was doing felt wonderful, but she wanted—she *needed*—more.

As if she'd spoken that need out loud, he dragged his lips back up along her throat, over her ear, jaw and chin, then finally covered her mouth again. Sabrina opened to receive him, and he tasted her deeply and thoroughly.

As he did, he dropped his hands to her waist again and began to move her backward, toward his bed. Impatiently, the two of them tugged down the covers, then returned to their embrace. Zane pressed his big body into hers, urging them both down onto the mattress until Sabrina lay on her back, her head cushioned by the palm of his hand. He positioned his own body alongside her, draping a leg over hers until his thigh was pressed into that most intimate part of her. She gasped at the contact, and he took advantage of her response to kiss her passionately again.

A tremor of anticipation shook her as he crowded himself more insistently against her and unfastened the remaining buttons of her shirt. Deftly, he unhooked the front closure of her bra until she felt a whisper of warm air caressing her naked torso. He trailed a line of butterfly kisses down her neck, along her shoulder and collarbone, between her breasts and finally, finally over one tender peak. He opened his mouth wide over her nipple and sucked deeply, the erotic pressure of his lips and tongue almost more than she could bear.

Oh. That felt…delicious. She wove her fingers through his silky hair to urge him closer still, silently begging for more. So Zane gave her more. He licked the undersides of her breasts with long, lingering strokes, taunted the stiff peaks with the tip of his tongue. With every taste, he pushed a hand lower, completely unzipping her jeans to dip his fingers inside, skimming along the waistband of her panties.

Sabrina was so focused on enjoying the pleasure she was feeling that she didn't pay attention to where his seemingly aimless wandering was taking him. Not until he pushed his hand beneath the silky fabric of her panties and buried his fingers in the damp, delicate folds of flesh between her legs. At that, she cried out, clenching her hands more tightly in his hair.

He paused his caresses at her response, as if awaiting a signal from her whether he should stop or continue. When her gaze found his, though, he was giving her a predatory little smile that told her he was enjoying himself as much as she was. She gave him a single, silent nod that she was having a good time, too, then she felt the fingers pressed against her moving again. Slowly, gently, two of them scissoring that most sensitive part of her before dipping inside to penetrate her. Her eyes fluttered closed at the contact, and her breathing grew shallow. Zane moved his fingers again, backward, forward, left, right, drawing erotic circles before thrusting his fingers inside again, more deeply.

"Oh, Zane…" she whispered. "Oh, that feels so… Oh…"

She heard his rough chuckle but couldn't quite bring herself to open her eyes. She remembered now what an attentive lover he'd been that night. He'd taken his time with her, touching her in ways she'd never been touched before, making her feel as if it was her first time all over again. And although this wasn't their first time, it did feel new. Like a new beginning for both of them. A do-over of sorts. And wow, was he doing it over well.

Vaguely, Sabrina registered the removal of her jeans, panties and sandals. She sensed Zane removing his clothing, too, then drawing near again. But there was nothing vague about her response when, instead of returning his fingers to the damp, pulsing core of her, his mouth went there instead. Her eyes snapped open wide, her fingers tangled in the sheets and she cried out again at the waves crashing through her when he flicked his tongue against her. All she could do after that was feel. Feel and marvel at the tremors and emotions wheeling through her, until they shattered into a billion shards of joy.

She called his name at her completion and pulled him up and into her arms. Clutching his shoulders, she clung to him for long moments. Before she could say anything, though—not that she had any idea what to say, since her brain had turned to pudding—he nestled himself between her legs and coaxed them wider still. She opened to him completely, wrapped her fingers around his long, rigid shaft and guided him to where they both wanted him to be.

He entered her with agonizing slowness, allowing her to acclimate her body to his. Sabrina drew her knees up toward herself, pressing the heels of her feet into the bed. Farther and farther Zane pushed himself, until he was buried as deep as he could be. He seemed to be everywhere inside her, filling places she hadn't realized were empty, heating parts of her she hadn't realized had cooled. For a moment, he stilled himself braced atop her, his gaze locked with hers. Then he withdrew and drove himself forward again. And she knew in that moment that Zane would never, ever leave those places inside her that he had claimed.

After that, she gave up thinking at all, because his movements became more rapid, more insistent. Again and again, he buried himself inside her, deeper and faster and harder. She bucked her hips upward to meet every thrust, wrapped her legs and arms tightly around him, until their damp, heated bodies seemed to fuse. Just when she was certain the two of them had indeed become one, his pumping ceased, his body went rigid atop hers, and he spilled himself inside her.

He turned their bodies so that she was atop him and kissed her again. First passionately, then gradually with more tenderness, a gentle denouement to their fierce climax. She dropped her hand to his chest and opened it over his heart, only to find it still beating as rapidly and raggedly as her own. It took a few moments for both of them to find their way back to the here and now. And when they did, all they could do was turn to look at the other and smile. Somehow, she knew they were both thinking the same thing. That this time, they weren't going to screw it up. They were going to do everything right. Because this time, they had more than themselves to think about.

That, she also knew, was why this time was even more amazing than the first. And she couldn't wait until they could do it again.

Chapter Ten

Zane was almost afraid to open his eyes the morning after his second night with Sabrina. He didn't want to awaken and discover that she had taken off again without saying goodbye. So instead, he slowly moved his hand across the top of the mattress until it connected with warm, soft, naked flesh. Immediately, he opened his eyes. There, in the soft early dawn light tumbling through his bedroom window, was Sabrina. Still asleep on her side facing him, her arm stretched toward him, her knuckles just shy of skimming his chest.

The euphoria that curled through him at seeing her there was almost more than he could stand. He covered her hand with his and lifted it to his mouth, then, one by one, kissed each of her fingertips. She stirred and smiled sleepily, then opened her eyes, too. He was afraid she might panic when she realized where she was and remembered what they had done last night. Instead, she lifted her other hand to push a few errant strands of blond from her eyes and smiled some more.

"Good morning," she murmured.

Oh, it was definitely that. "Good morning."

"What time is it?"

The right time, he wanted to reply. The perfect time. He glanced at the clock, then back at a delightfully sleep-rumpled Sabrina. "Not even seven," he said. "Sleep some more if you want. Night Heron Ranch is a pretty lazy place on Saturdays. And the boys probably won't be up till almost noon."

She winced at that. "They must have seen my car still here when they came home last night. And they must have seen that your bedroom door was closed."

"Yeah." Zane grinned. "And they must have realized that their plan last night worked exactly the way they wanted it to."

She winced again, but it was followed by a smile.

"They're big boys now, Sabrina," he reminded her. "They know what goes on between two consenting adults who are—" He stopped himself before revealing too much. Just how exactly *did* he feel about Sabrina, anyway? "Who are having a baby together," he finally finished saying.

She didn't seem to notice his hesitation. Instead, she scooched herself closer to him and opened her hand over the center of his chest. Beneath it, his heart started pounding wildly, just from a simple touch. He wanted to make love to her again. And then again after that. In fact, he wanted to spend the entire day in bed with her. Would there ever come a time when he'd had his fill of Sabrina Fortune?

"Last night was amazing," he told her.

She nodded. "Yeah, it was. Even better than the first time."

He wondered why that was. Seemed like the first

time two people came together would always be the best. Especially a one-night stand—all the steamy excitement and taboo naughtiness of two virtual strangers coming together in the most intimate way possible. But she was right. Knowing more about her, spending time with her, sharing something besides sex with her, all of that had brought something more to the experience. Had made it even more intimate. Was it going to be even better next time? Then better the time after that?

And why was he suddenly looking forward to a lot of *next times* with Sabrina? It had been ages since he'd wanted a woman as much as he wanted her. Hell, he didn't think he'd ever wanted a woman as much as he did her. But especially since swearing off romance and love and all those things a person couldn't trust, he really hadn't looked forward to spending so much time with a woman. Now, though…

Well, now he was beginning to wonder if he'd been a bit hasty in dismissing all the love and romance stuff.

"We should do it again," she said, smiling.

Well, okay then. He bent his head to hers for a kiss.

"I mean when your brothers aren't right up the hall," she said with a chuckle.

He kissed her, anyway. Just a brief, chaste one, since anything else would have definitely led to what she didn't want to do in a full house, but it was still enough to get his motor revving.

"But we should definitely do it again," she repeated when he pulled away.

"The boys are all going to be driving or flying back to their respective schools tomorrow," he said. "And

Astrid's off on Sundays. Got any plans for tomorrow night?"

She cupped her hand over his cheek. "Only to spend it with you."

"It's a date then," he said.

She smiled. "Our first."

Oh, wow, she was right. They'd technically known each other for months, had made love twice and they still hadn't been on a proper date, just the two of them.

"We really didn't go about this in the right order, did we?" he said.

She shook her head. "But we're getting there, anyway."

They were getting somewhere, that was for sure. And they both seemed to be on the same path toward approaching it. Just where exactly *it* was, though… That remained to be seen. But at this moment, it felt pretty damned good.

"Come on," he said. "Let's get dressed and go downstairs. I'll fix you and our daughters a big ranch breakfast."

They had finished eating and were working on their second cups of decaf—Astrid had stocked up after Zane told her about Sabrina's prenatal sacrifice—when his phone pinged with a text about something he hadn't thought about for weeks. A text from his attorney that simply said, All done. You're good to go. Zane should have been delighted by the message. Instead, his heart sank, and a hole opened up in the pit of his stomach. Talk about bad timing.

"What's wrong?" Sabrina asked from her seat beside him.

He glanced up quickly. "What? Oh, nothing's wrong. Just some business I've had going on has been settled, that's all."

"On a Saturday?" she asked. "I didn't realize you were such a workaholic."

"I'm not," he assured her. "I thought it was going to be a while yet, before this was tied up." He forced a smile he was nowhere close to feeling. "Guess someone's doing business over a round of golf or something."

She didn't look anywhere near convinced. "You don't look like a man who's happy to have some business taken care of. You look like a kid who just found out there's no Santa Claus."

He laughed, but even he could hear the distress in the sound. "That's crazy. Santa Claus is totally real."

She didn't return his laugh. Didn't even chuckle. She did smile, but it didn't look any more genuine than the one he tried to force.

"Okay, so anyway," he interjected, "how do you want to spend the weekend? Before our first date tomorrow night?"

Her anxious expression cleared—some—and she opened her mouth to reply. But her phone started ringing somewhere in the room. She looked over at where she'd left her purse the evening before. The tightness in his chest clenched harder. He wanted to tell her not to answer it, since he was pretty sure he knew what that call was about. She seemed to sense his fear, because instead of ignoring her phone, she strode slowly over to withdraw it from the side pocket of her purse. He found some relief in the fact that the phone stopped ringing before she could get it out.

That relief evaporated, however, when he heard her say, "That's weird. It was my Realtor."

He was hoping she'd say something about calling back later, since, hey, Sabrina wasn't a workaholic, either, so why would she want to do business on a weekend? Instead, she pressed the button to return the call just as an alert dinged to let her know there was a voicemail.

"Hi, Dasha, it's Sabrina," she said when the recipient picked up on the other end. "Sorry I missed your call. I couldn't get to my phone in time. What's up? I didn't play the voicemail yet."

Naturally Zane couldn't hear what Sabrina's Realtor was telling her over the phone. But he didn't have to. He knew exactly what she was telling her. That the parcel of lakefront land she'd been so sure was hers, the property she was supposed to be closing on in less than a month, upon which she wanted to build a grief camp for people coping with the loss of a loved one, had just been deemed a possession of the Baston family. Turned out that the sale his great-grandfather had completed with the previous owner had never been legal in the first place, and now it had been rightfully returned to the person who should have inherited it by now—Zane Baston. Not necessarily because of any legal loopholes, but because the old boy network of Chatelaine, Texas, of which the Bastons of Chatelaine had been members since the town's founding, had worked the way it always did, favoring one of its members instead of the upstart new kid in town.

Never before had Zane felt more terrible about getting exactly what he wanted.

"Uh-huh," Sabrina was saying into her phone on the other side of the room.

She had her back to him, though, so he had no way to register her feelings. Not that he really needed to discern those. He was pretty sure he knew exactly what she was feeling.

"I see," she said. Evenly. Coolly. Like someone plotting murder. "And there's nothing we can do?" She listened some more then said, "No, I appreciate what you did, Dasha, I really do. I know how these things go, though. God knows the business world is full of stuff like this. And my father was an absolute master of the corporate double-cross."

At this, she finally did turn around to look at Zane. And if looks could kill, he would have been dismembered on the spot, and his body parts set on fire. With a flamethrower.

"Listen, I'll have to call you back," she said to Dasha. "I'm not at home right now, but I will be in a matter of minutes. Maybe we can regroup and figure out something else." Very pointedly, she asked her Realtor, "Do you know a good attorney? One who's an absolute shark?" After a second, she replied, "Great. Text me her number."

Then she was disconnecting. And glaring at Zane some more. He wished he knew what to say to defuse the situation. Unfortunately, the bomb had already detonated, so it was moot.

"How dare you?" she said evenly. "That land was mine. I was supposed to close next month."

"Sabrina, I—"

"That camp was my dream, Zane. And you knew it."

"I know, but—"

"How *could* you?"

He waited to see if she would actually pause long enough for him to respond to her charges, and when she did, he pointed out, "You can put your camp anywhere, Sabrina. And your family's ranch is a couple thousand acres at least. Plenty of room. I need that access to the lake to keep my animals alive."

"You can revive your pond," she reminded him. "It isn't that hard. I need access to the lake, too, because water has healing properties, and I was going to build an area for meditation and contemplation on the water."

"Your family's ranch abuts the lake. Use some of that."

"I can't. That part of the ranch is where our houses are. My siblings support my vision for the grief camp, but I don't think they'd like having it right outside their window with all the activity it's going to generate. And I don't blame them. And anyway," she said, hurrying on when he was going to object again, "that's beside the point. The point is that you went behind my back and used some shady business tactics to steal that land from me. And you've been lying to me for weeks."

Actually, it was his attorney who did the shady business tactics, he wanted to say. Problem was, he'd done it with Zane's blessing. But that was before he realized it was Sabrina he was competing with. He'd thought it was some faceless Fortune newcomer to town who'd never made any kind of contribution to Chatelaine and felt like they could just take whatever they wanted. Then again, he hadn't exactly backed off once he *did* discover it was Sabrina who'd snapped up the land he wanted, had he? No, it had been business as usual. He'd just felt kind of bad about doing it, where before he wouldn't have felt anything at all.

"I need that land, Sabrina," he told her. It was the only leg he had to stand on.

"You lied to me," she said again. "And you stole from me. And all the while you were acting like you cared about me."

"I do care about you."

Hell, he more than cared about her. He just hadn't quite figured out what, exactly, that *more* was.

"If you cared about me, you would have been honest with me. And you wouldn't have taken something you knew is important to me."

A door opened upstairs, and Zane heard Cody's voice calling out to his brothers, asking who wanted waffles, because he was going to make some. Sabrina heard him, too. With one final scowl for Zane, she stuffed her phone back into her purse and slung it over her shoulder.

"Any other business you and I have will be going through our lawyers," she told him. "And that includes where Peach and Plum are concerned. Don't ever contact me or speak to me again."

"Oh, Sabrina, no," he said. "No. We can work this out. We just need to talk about it. Tomorrow night, after the boys are gone."

As if to illustrate how very much she meant what she just said, she turned her back on him again and made her way out of the dining room. Zane followed her, doing his best to convince her that he hadn't done anything wrong, that she just needed to see his side of things to understand that it was just business, and that they could work this out. *Please*. But she only hastened her step, wrenched open the front door and passed through it. She thumbed the fob for her car to unlock it, climbed inside and locked the doors behind herself. Then, without giving him another glance, she threw the vehicle in gear and drove away. And all Zane could do was stand there, left in the literal dust kicked up by her car, and wonder how in the hell he was going to fix things this time.

He awoke the next morning to a head full of confusion and fear. He'd spent the entire day after Sabrina stormed off veering between panicking about the fracture in their relationship and pretending for his brothers that there was absolutely nothing wrong. He told them the reason for her absence was that she had just had some family stuff to see to, and she was sorry she couldn't be there to send the boys back off to school. Then he'd told himself he might very well have screwed up so badly this time that there was no way to fix it.

There had to be a way to fix it. Unfortunately, he'd spent so much of the night tossing and turning and fearful and fretful that he couldn't seem to piece together a coherent thought.

Desperate times called for desperate measures, he finally decided. There was only one person in Chatelaine he could turn to at a time like this. Fortunately, he knew exactly where to find the guy. Beau Weatherly had been handing out his Free Life Advice for years at the coffee shop, and from what Zane had heard, he'd never steered anyone wrong with his guidance. Hell, the guy knew pretty much everything about everything. Living a life as long and full as his gave a person the kind of insight Zane could only hope he acquired someday. Beau would surely know what to do to help him out, too.

He looked at the clock on the nightstand. It was almost 8:00. Beau was at the Daily Grind every morning between 7:00 and 8:30 a.m. to dish out his pearls of wisdom. Zane was going to have to hurry.

But when he made it into Chatelaine, he was dismayed to see a host of cars parked at the Daily Grind. He jumped out of his truck and raced into the coffee shop, then was relieved to see Beau still sitting at his table. His iced coffee was almost empty, and all that was left of his scone was crumbs. There was no line to talk to him, though, and the woman who was with him now was standing up and shaking his hand. Before Beau could get up, too, Zane hurried to his table and sat down in the chair the woman had left empty only seconds before.

Beau would stay long enough to talk to him, Zane knew. He'd lost his wife five years ago after nursing her through a long illness, and he'd dealt with his grief by being a friend to everyone in Chatelaine. His Free Life Advice table was the culmination of that. The guy's insights were both generous and priceless.

"Morning, Zane," Beau said. "Figured I'd be seeing

you at some point. Kinda thought it would be before now, though."

Zane dipped his head in greeting but said nothing. His brain was too full of thoughts zipping around and not landing anywhere. He had no idea where to start explaining things to the other man, especially with only— He glanced at his watch. Hell. There was only six minutes left of the life guru's time. He looked at Beau Weatherly again, at his kind dark eyes and the way his thick, silvering dark hair fell carelessly forward on his head. Zane hoped he held up as well as this guy when he was in his sixties.

"I gather this has something to do with Sabrina Fortune," Beau said. "Been hearing a lot of chatter about you two."

Zane nodded again. But he still said nothing. It was like every word he knew was suddenly foreign to him. Beau studied him expectantly for some minutes more, but he didn't say anything, either. Finally, he picked up his iced coffee and drained what little was left. Then he wadded up the scone crumbs in his napkin. He was giving Zane time to sort his thoughts. Problem was, Zane couldn't light on a single thought long enough to voice it.

"You know, silence can be very noisy," Beau finally told him. "What I'm hearing from yours is that you already know the answer to your predicament. Just do what's in your heart, not your stubborn head. You have a good heart, Zane. It's already trying to tell you what you need to do. You should listen."

And with that, Beau picked up the Stetson sitting on the table beside him and stood. Then he collected the remnants of his breakfast to toss on his way out and left. Zane watched, open-mouthed as the older man sauntered toward the exit, frankly kind of shocked by what Beau had just said.

Or, rather, didn't say. This was the *great life advice* he'd wanted and needed? That he already knew the answer to his problem? Beau was supposed to guide him through the steps on how to fix his problems with Sabrina. Tell him everything he needed to do to make things between the two of them okay. Like maybe how Zane needed to apologize for misleading her about the land, even if he hadn't done it intentionally. And get him to admit that he could have been wrong to do that. Then Beau could have helped him see that it would have been better to have considered her feelings on the matter and understand just how important her grief camp was to her. Like maybe, you know, communicate with her. See if there was some way they could reach a compromise.

And maybe, just maybe, how he should tell her he was pretty sure he'd fallen in love with her over the past few weeks. And how he couldn't imagine living without her.

Oh. Okay. So maybe Beau was right. Maybe Zane already did know the answer. But it created a whole new problem. How were he and Sabrina supposed to communicate their feelings and compromise on a piece of land when she was convinced he was a liar and a creep?

First things first, Zane thought. Apologize to Sabrina. Somehow. And acknowledge—oh, boy, this wasn't going to be easy—that he was...wrong. There. He said it. In his head, anyway. Now he just had to figure out how to get the words out of his mouth. Most of all, though, he had to tell her how much he loved her. How he wanted to spend the rest of his life with her. With her and their daughters. Like a real family.

No. Not *like* a family. *As* a family. A real, honest-to-God family. That was what he wanted with Sabrina. He would say—and do—whatever it took to make her believe that.

And he hoped like hell that, at least on some level, she felt the same way about him, too.

Chapter Eleven

Sabrina was poring over columns of numbers at the Fortune Family Ranch offices a few days after telling Zane to figuratively jump in the lake he'd stolen from her when she started feeling sick. Nothing major, really, just a little nausea that she told herself was due to the leftover gazpacho she'd had for lunch, even though she'd barely touched it because it had been too spicy for her liking. This in spite of the fact that she'd made it herself the night before, and she hadn't been able to get it spicy enough then. Last night, the growing babies inside her had loved the extra kick. Today, evidently, not so much. She popped an antacid and went back to the numbers on the spreadsheet she'd opened on her desktop and tried to ignore how fuzzy they suddenly seemed. But she couldn't quite help dropping a hand to splay it open over her belly.

She was starting to show now, even if only she—and, okay, Zane, during that night they spent together—were able to see it. To the outside world, she looked like her usual self. She was still wearing her regular clothes, just not pulling the zippers up all the way on her skirts and pants, and she was opting for the oversize shirts she normally saved for weekends relaxing at home, letting them hang untucked. It was fashionable, she assured herself. It was.

Her phone pinged with an alert, but she didn't bother picking it up. She was sure it was a text from Zane. Again. He'd been texting and calling for days, apologizing and telling her they needed to talk. That he could explain. That they could work things out. Yes, she knew all along that the two of them had been at odds over that land. But she'd thought after all they talked about, when he finally understood how much it meant to her, he'd back off. Instead, he'd dug in more deeply. How could she work things out with someone who had so blatantly lied to her? Lied to her while romancing her? While making her fall in love with him?

Because Sabrina had fallen in love with Zane. She knew that. It was why his deception and betrayal hurt so badly. That morning at his house, after spending her second night with him, she'd awakened feeling so... wonderful. So complete. So happy. As if nothing in her life could ever go wrong again. And even if somehow it did, then she would have Zane there to help her through it.

The way they'd had breakfast together that morning, as if it were something they did every day... She'd been thinking it would be something they did do every day after that. First together, then with their daughters. That morning, she'd just felt like her entire life had moved around a corner and found nothing but perfection on the other side.

Perfection. Ha. Never had she found herself in such

a mess. There was no way she and Zane could work through this. But there was no way she could erase him from her life.

Another pain shot through her belly, and she told herself again it was nothing but too spicy of a lunch. Until the discomfort grew worse over the next thirty minutes. And then even worse after that. Maybe if she got up and moved around a little bit, it would level off. Pushing her chair away from the desk, she rose to standing. Then immediately had to grip the edge of the desk to steady herself. Woo. She was lightheaded, too. Must have risen too fast. Once the dizziness passed, she released her grip and took a step away from the desk.

Okay, good. She didn't fall. Carefully, she placed one foot in front of the other to make her way across her office to the door. It should have been an easy trek, considering the room was only about ten feet by eight feet due to it originally being a child's bedroom in the house the first owners had built back in the fifties. The Fortunes had thought it would be perfect for the ranch offices, with just enough rooms to give each sibling their own workspace. But even after walking the small distance between her desk and the hallway, Sabrina was nearly worn out, and she was having trouble catching her breath.

She gripped the doorjamb on each side and looked down the hall of what she couldn't help thinking was an impossibly small house for a family by today's standards. With measured steps, and still pressing her hand against one wall for balance, she walked past Dahlia's office, past her brother Arlo's, past Jade's and Ridge's offices, all the way to her brother Nash's—the largest office, since he was their ranch foreman. Then she turned to pace back again. Okay, that was better. Her head was starting to clear, and her breathing was returning to normal.

Until she started feeling stabbing pains in her lower torso that felt like someone was dragging a knife through her midsection. That was when she started to panic.

Opening her hand over her womb again, she managed to make her way to her desk, where she'd left her phone. Somehow, she was able to punch in Dahlia's number, and when her sister answered, she could describe the episode she was having. Vaguely, she heard her twin say she was on her way over. Then she dropped her phone as she crumpled to the floor. And then...then everything went black.

Zane was busy inspecting the fence line of his ranch before inclement weather starting setting in—it would take a while to cover the entire circumference of five square miles of ranch—when he heard his phone ringing in his back pocket. Damn. He had a foot of barbed wire wrapped around one gloved hand, and the other was steadying a fence post. No way could he answer, as desperately as he wanted to. What if it was Sabrina? Finally?

Then again, it was highly unlikely that she would be calling him. He must have texted her a hundred times over the last few days and left nearly that many messages. She'd completely ignored him. He told himself to give her time and space, that with a little more of both, she'd eventually come around. Maybe not to forgiving him just yet, but to at least talking to him. And once they talked, maybe she'd finally be able to forgive him. And then hopefully the two of them could work things out.

Whoever was trying to get ahold of him now was doubtless one of those "spam likely" calls. He wasn't even concerned when his phone pinged to alert him that the number left a voicemail. His car warranty was up-to-date, he hadn't applied for any loans that he might be eligible to receive an even larger amount for, his taxes were all paid and he didn't know a single member of the Nigerian royal family.

But when the phone rang two more times, followed by two more voicemail notifications and then a half dozen text alerts sounded after that, he hastily finished his fence patching job and tugged his phone out of his pocket. Maybe Sabrina needed him after all. The calls and texts came from two different numbers, however, neither of which was Sabrina's. And neither of which he recognized, though both had Texas area codes. What got his attention, though, were two words in each of the texts that appeared on his home screen: Sabrina and hospital. That was when he stripped off his gloves and unlocked his phone to read the texts in full.

Each was from one of Sabrina's sisters, and all of them were frantic. He was hurrying toward his buck-skin quarter horse, Hawkeye, before he even finished reading them. The gist of it was that Dahlia had found Sabrina unconscious in her office after her sister called her complaining of abdominal pain, and now all three Fortune women were on their way to the ER at County

General Hospital. Panic-stricken, Zane launched himself onto Hawkeye and raced him with all the speed of
a Thoroughbred back to the barn. He left the horse with
Mateo to cool him off, hurriedly explaining that Sabrina
was in the hospital, then he ran out again. He was barely
thinking as he jumped into his truck and raced off to
County General, his head too full of what-ifs to make
sense of anything but his fear.

He found Dahlia and Jade in the ER on the edge of
their seats, both looking as haggard and worried as he
felt. When they saw him enter, they both jumped up
and began talking at once, so furiously that Zane could
hardly understand a word.

"Stop," he said, holding up a hand. "I'm not following either one of you."

Both exchanged a quick look, then Jade deferred to
Dahlia, who began to explain again.

"Sabrina called me about an hour ago to tell me she
was having abdominal pains, and she passed out in the
middle of the conversation. She was able to say she was
at the ranch office, though, so I drove over there and
found her unconscious in front of her desk. She woke
up shortly after that, but was still really lightheaded.
Jade and I both had to help her walk into the ER when
we got here." She gestured toward a door on the other
side of the room. "They took her in back in a wheelchair
and she's been there ever since."

Jade nodded. "We were able to sit with her for a little
bit, but then they took her off to run some tests. They
didn't want to do an X-ray because of the twins, so

they're doing an MRI. Also another ultrasound to make sure the babies are okay. And maybe some other stuff."

Zane wasn't crazy about the fact that Sabrina had called her sister instead of him, though he guessed he understood, all things considered. But when it came to their babies, he kinda hoped she would put all their issues aside. Still, he was here now, and he sure as hell wasn't leaving this time until he saw her. He just hoped and prayed she and their babies were all okay.

"Did they say how long it was going to take?" he asked the sisters.

They both shook their heads.

Jade said, "I've never known a hospital to be particularly speedy, though."

Neither had Zane.

"There's a coffee shop around the corner if you want something to eat while we're waiting."

Right. Like he could stomach anything at the moment.

"Nah, I'll just wait with you two if you don't mind."

Now both nodded. Sabrina had canceled the dinner he was supposed to attend to formally meet her family, but he had no idea what kind of explanation she'd given them for doing it. Her sisters weren't exactly being warm and fuzzy, though—not that a situation like this called for that—so he sensed they at least knew he was the one who'd screwed up. Still, maybe Sabrina hadn't told them about the specifics of their argument. Or, if she had, her sisters knew something like that had no place in what could potentially be a life-or-death situation.

No, Zane immediately censured himself. Whatever

was going on with Sabrina and the babies, it was *not* life or death. He wasn't about to put that kind of thinking out into the world and invite God knew what back in. Sabrina was going to be fine. So were Peach and Plum. Her doctor was going to figure out what was wrong—which was nothing major, he assured himself again—and then treat it, and everything would be back to normal. He and Sabrina could talk through their differences and fix whatever was wrong between them, too. *Healing.* That was what this day was going to bring. For everything.

What felt like days later, the ER doctor finally came out to talk to them. It heartened Zane that he recognized her from high school—Sofia López had been a few years ahead of him but had been inarguably the smartest kid at Chatelaine High. He'd heard she came back to her hometown to practice and was super relieved to know someone like her had been caring for Sabrina. He was even more grateful to see that she was smiling as she approached them. Her dark hair was cropped short, and her oversize glasses were the same purple color as her scrubs.

"Hello, I'm Dr. López." She introduced herself to Dahlia and Jade when she stopped in front of them. She smiled at Zane. "We went to school together, yes?"

He nodded. "Zane Baston."

"Right. Good to see you." Then she cut to the chase. "Sabrina is going to be fine. The pain she was feeling in her lower abdomen was, believe it or not, indigestion. It had nothing to do with the twins she's carrying. They're dancing around in there like they're listening to Selena singing 'Bidi Bidi Bom Bom.' So no worries on that."

"What caused her to faint?" Zane asked gruffly.

At this, Dr. López tsked. "The fainting came after *some*one—someone who's pregnant with twins and should know better—said she skipped breakfast this morning because she had a very important business call, and then only ate half a bowl of soup for lunch. Sabrina also said she hasn't been sleeping well the past few nights and has been stressing over some things in her personal life. It was a perfect storm for something like this to happen."

Not sleeping well, Zane echoed to himself. Stressing over personal things. Yeah, well, that made two of them.

"I think this was a wake-up call for her, though," the doctor continued. "She's promised she's going to take it easier and pay more attention to her eating and sleeping habits." Now she looked at Zane. "She also said she'd like to talk to you. Presuming you're the…let me think how she put it…" She feigned deep thought, then said, "I remember now. The tall, dark-haired, good-looking, stubborn, unreasonable, insufferable, but still kind of okay guy, even if he can't understand the most basic things about how relationships are supposed to work." She grinned. "Or something like that. Anyway, she's in room 217."

Zane started grinning at the word *stubborn*. Sounded like Sabrina was finally coming around. *Stubborn*, *unreasonable* and *insufferable* were way better than some of the things she'd called him last time they were together.

Dahlia looked like she wanted to object that Sabrina had asked for Zane before her sisters, but Jade put a hand on her shoulder and squeezed gently. "I think Zane seeing Sabrina first is a good idea," she said. "Don't you, Dahlia? Don't you think it's good that Sabrina wants to talk to Zane before she talks to us?"

It took a minute, but Dahlia's expression gradually changed from displeased to begrudging contentment. "Why, yes," she agreed. "Yes, Jade, I think that's very good. Go ahead, Zane. We'll just grab a bite at the café and talk to Sabrina in a bit."

Zane offered them both a grateful smile in return, murmured his thanks to the doctor, then headed off to find room 217.

Sabrina had finished her dinner of yummy hospital food—chicken potpie, creamed spinach, fried green tomatoes, biscuit with butter and chocolate cake, all of which she figured were going to send her straight to the cardiac ward if she had to stay here more than one night—when she looked up to see Zane standing at the entrance to her room. Damn. Right when she was lifting the last bite of that chocolate cake to her mouth, too, after assuring him she was cutting out sweets while she was pregnant. As subtly as she could, she lowered the forkful of cake back onto her place. Then, as *un*subtly as she could, she glared at him.

"I'm not speaking to you," she said.

Even if, she had to admit, it was really nice to see him. She'd been terrified when she woke up on her office floor with Dahlia trying to rouse her. The panic in her sister's eyes had just made it worse. All the way to the hospital, all Sabrina had been able to think about were her daughters and Zane. Telling herself over and over again that the babies were going to be fine, and berating herself for cutting ties with their father over something the two of them could surely work through if they just tried communicating. As much as she'd appreciated Dahlia being with her, and then Jade when her other sister arrived at the hospital the same time they did, the person Sabrina had really wanted to be with was Zane.

She was still angry with him. But she was still in love with him, too. And one of those emotions, she had come to realize, was definitely stronger than the other.

"Sure sounds like you're speaking to me," he replied, biting back a smile.

"Only long enough to tell you I'm not speaking to you."

"So you spoke."

This time he didn't even try to hide his grin. But it was one filled with relief, as if he were thanking every star in the universe that she and the babies were okay. And that she was talking to him instead of throwing things at him.

He nodded toward the cake she'd tried to hide. "So much for cutting back on sugar."

Instead of feeling guilty, she shot him a look of triumph. "Dr. López said it's fine. That the occasional sweet is part of a balanced diet, not to mention a fun treat, as long as I don't overdo it. You're just trying to be a big bossy know-it-all."

Instead of looking offended, he just grinned wider. "Hey, I don't mind at all. That means I can go back to

enjoying Astrid's havreflarns again." This time he nodded toward the coffee cup that she'd also been gifted
with for dinner. "What's Dr. López say about caffeine?"

It had been excellent enough to find out that she and
the babies were perfectly fine. The chocolate cake thing
had just been, well, icing. But the good news had just
kept coming today. "Caffeine is also fine in modera-
tion," she informed him.

She might as well have just told Zane he won another
billion dollar lottery. "Oh, thank God," he said.

"What? I thought you loved the ginger pomegranate
tea at the Daily Grind."

"Oh, yeah," he said with the kind of enthusiasm that
was clearly... What was that word? Oh, yeah. *Fake.*
"Yeah, that ginger pomegranate tea was awesome. But,
you know, coffee is even more awesome."

She couldn't disagree. As much as she liked herbal
tea, it really didn't do anything to promote coherency.
And she liked coherency even better. Her dinner coffee,
though, wasn't why she was feeling so coherent now.
That was due to the still-too-fresh-in-her-memory hor-
ror she'd experienced that afternoon, fearing she was
about to lose everything.

"I'm sorry I haven't answered any of your texts or
calls," she said without preamble.

"I'm sorry I lied to you," Zane replied just as reso-
lutely.

"Then why did you?"

He expelled a soft sigh. "Because I honestly kind of
forgot all about the land thing once you told me about
the pregnancy thing."

"How could you forget it when I kept bringing it up?"

"Because it wasn't me handling the transaction. It was my attorney. And he's more about getting things accomplished than he is about telling me what he's doing."

"But you knew he was trying to get the land for you," she said.

"I did."

"And you knew he was going to resort to nefarious means to get it."

"I did not," he replied.

"Oh, come on, Zane. You said you were being honest."

"I am, Sabrina, I swear."

He took a few steps into the room, then hesitated, as if he still wasn't sure of his reception. Sabrina wasn't too sure of his reception yet, either. But she did kind of wish he would move a little closer.

"Look," he began, sounding almost as tired as she was, "back when I thought I was dealing with a stranger who wanted that land, I told my attorney to do whatever it took to get it for me. But I meant whatever was *ethical*. I had no idea he'd skirt the issue to make it happen. And hell, for all I knew, there really was a problem with the provenance, and the land really did still belong to my family. I have to talk to him—*we* have to talk to him," he quickly said, clarifying. "And even more important, we have to talk to each other."

She studied him in silence. A few weeks ago, she wouldn't have believed him. But back then, she hadn't really known him. Now, though… She let her anger go. Sabrina knew Zane was a good person. She knew he was decent. But more than that, she knew she loved him. And she wouldn't be able to do that if he was the kind of man who could woo a woman from one side and steal what he knew was important to her from the other.

He took a few more steps into the room, then stopped, looking like he still wasn't sure of his reception. And although Sabrina would have preferred receiving him just about anywhere but the hospital—and wearing just about anything but an ugly blue hospital gown—she was so happy to see him in that moment that she really didn't care much about anything else. He was right. They did need to talk. A lot. So she lowered the side rail on her bed between her and him, scooted over as much as she could, patting the mattress beside her. She didn't have to ask twice. Zane made his way across the room and perched on the edge.

He looked wonderful, she couldn't help thinking, all scruffy and unshaven, his blue work shirt and jeans streaked with dirt, as if he'd rushed to the hospital from whatever he'd been doing on the ranch without giving a thought to his appearance. His eyes, though, those gorgeous green eyes, were shadowed and exhausted-looking, as if, like her, he hadn't been getting much sleep.

"We should probably talk about what happened the last time we were together," he said softly.

She shook her head. "No. I don't want to talk about that. It was stupid, and it's in the past, and it's not important anymore. It's not the thing that matters most."

He looked relieved, but not quite convinced that it wasn't important anymore. "Well, what is important now?" he asked. "What does matter most?"

She reached for his hand and twined her fingers with his. Then she moved both to her belly and splayed them open over it and each other. "This," she said. "This is what matters. The babies we created and will be guiding through life, together." She smiled. "At least until they're grown-ups. Then we'll have to pretend we're letting them guide themselves. But we'll always be there with them, Zane. For them. And we need to focus on that."

He pressed his hand gently against her tummy, then turned it so that his palm was pressed against hers. Then he laced their fingers together and closed his hand over hers.

"I think we need to focus on us, too," he told her.

And the way he said it made something inside Sabrina melt into a mass of...so many things. Relief. Happiness. Devotion. Love. She really did love this man. Loved him in a way she'd never loved anyone else. With Preston, her love had always been young and innocent and unsophisticated. First love. Young love. Love two people shared for each other and no one else.

But with Zane, it was so much different.

Sabrina had learned so much in the past decade, about life and herself. She'd experienced the gamut of emotions, both good and bad, and come out on the other side with a much better understanding of just what it meant to love and understand someone else and commit your whole heart to that person. And not just Zane, but Peach and Plum, too. The four of them were irrevocably intertwined. Whatever she had to do, whatever sacrifices and concessions she had to make, she would. Because she knew Zane would do the same for her. They could fix whatever was wrong between them. She knew they could. And it would only make them stronger in the long run, and able to handle everything else that was going to come at them after their daughters were born.

She got that now. All the antagonism between them, all the frustration, all the misunderstanding… It had all been a part of learning about each other. And teaching each other, too. Because on some level, somewhere deep inside themselves, they'd realized they were going to be together, in one way or another, forever. Their hearts had realized that, even if their heads hadn't yet. It had become so clear to her today, when she'd feared she was going to lose it all. But she didn't know how to tell Zane that now.

"I think we need to focus on us," he said again, "because *us*, you and me, is just as important as *them*, those babies we're going to be raising."

Tears pricked her eyes at the look on his face and the gentleness of his tone. But she still had no idea what to tell him. That was okay, though. Because Zane seemed to know exactly what to say.

"You know what I think?" he asked her. "About why you and I were never able to talk about co-parenting and how we always started but got sidetracked by something else?"

She shook her head. "No. Why?"

"I think the reason we always stopped talking about it almost as soon as we started is because, somehow, even without realizing it consciously, we both knew that we'd never be co-parenting at all."

She should have been alarmed by that. But the way

he was looking at her now was anything but alarming. Rather, it made all the fears and worries that were lingering inside her start to slowly wash away.

"We won't be co-parenting?" she asked.

He shook his head. "Nope. I think we both knew it wasn't our thing. I think instead we realized that what we were going to be doing was *parenting*. The way two people do when they love their offspring as much as they love each other and want to do what's best for the family they're creating together."

She expelled a soft sound as more tears pricked her eyes. "And do you love me, Zane?"

He nodded. "With all my heart."

"Then say it."

He smiled. "I love you, Sabrina Windham Fortune. With all my heart. And I don't want to lose you. I want to spend the rest of my life with you."

Wow. All she'd asked for was three little words. What she'd gotten in return was a life plan. One that she realized mirrored her own.

"I love you, too, Zane Baston. With all my heart. With all three hearts beating inside me right now."

She wasn't sure, but his eyes seemed to go a little damp at that. "Well, then, what say these four hearts join together to make one family?"

She squeezed his hand tight. "I think it's a good plan," she told him. Then, with mock seriousness, she added, "Just don't think this lets you off the hook. We still have a lot to talk about."

"We do," he agreed, his smile growing broader. "And the sooner we say what we need to say, the better."

Oh, Sabrina didn't know. She figured they'd said the most important stuff just now. Anything else they had to say would just be communication and compromise. But then, that was what being a family was all about, wasn't it? Well, those and love and respect. Mostly love, though. That was the part she liked best.

Funny, how she'd come to Chatelaine because of her Fortune family only to find a whole new one waiting here for her.

"I love you, Zane."

"I love you, Sabrina."

Together, they looked down at the little mound hidden under her hospital gown.

"We love you, too, Peach and Plum," she told their daughters.

Zane laughed. "And we can't wait to meet you."

Epilogue

Sabrina didn't think she'd ever seen more spectacular sunsets than the ones in east Texas. The sky above her was awash with pinks and golds and lavenders, colors that stretched and shimmered in their lake reflections. There must have been something about the curvature of the Earth here that just made the end of the day more beautiful. Or maybe it was just that the sunsets were happening in Texas, where everything was bigger and broader and better. Bigger and broader, too, was Sabrina, who had well and truly started to show in her sixteenth week of pregnancy. She'd even sprung for a few wardrobe pieces to accommodate the changes to her body that the two little girls growing inside her had brought. She loved her new maternity dress dotted with tiny bluebonnets. So much that she'd even tied a blue ribbon around the bottom of her loose braid to match them.

As for the better part…

She looked at the man beside her. Well, now. Zane was more than better. And he was going to be the best father in the world.

"You sure you're not marrying me for my land?" he asked, smiling.

"You mean *my* land," she countered.

"*Our* land," he corrected them both.

The land they were standing on right now, watching as the sun dipped low over the horizon. They'd be filing the paperwork for that later in the week, with no help from any old boys' networks or shark lawyers. Even though they'd set their wedding date for next summer so that their daughters could be there, too, they'd bought this parcel together and were making plans for it as a united front.

"Yeah, our land," she said. "And no, I'm not marrying you for that. I'm marrying you because I love you and can't live without you. Oh, and also because you're the father of my children."

"Well, that's gonna be handy," Zane said, "because I love you, too, and can't live without you, either. You or those little ones growing inside you."

He moved behind her, wrapping his arms around her waist to splay his hands open over her softly burgeoning belly. Automatically, she covered his hands with hers. A bright blue sapphire on her left ring finger glittered in the twilight when she did. Zane had bought it for her because he said it reminded him of that devil-in-the-blue-dress gown she'd been wearing the night they met.

"How y'all doing in there, Peach and Plum?" he asked their daughters as he skimmed his hand tenderly over her baby bump. "Got enough room to move around?"

Sabrina laughed. "If they don't, they'll just make

more. And then more. Will you still love me when I'm as big as Lake Chatelaine?"

He dipped his head to hers and brushed his lips over her cheek. "To distraction," he promised.

For a long moment, they only stared out at the lake and the sunset, each lost in their own thoughts. Finally, Sabrina said, "I'm thinking I'll put the Serenity Shelter right here where we're standing. Especially now that I've seen how breathtaking the sunset looks from here. What do you think?"

"Serenity Shelter," he repeated. "Is that what you're planning to call that part of the camp?"

She nodded. "I think it fits."

"I think you're right. And yes, this would be the perfect spot. Where are you going to put the rest of it?"

Since she already knew down to the square foot how she wanted the grief camp laid out, she told Zane exactly where she wanted to situate the textile lab, the education station, the loom room and a small pen to house some of Dahlia's sheep for a one-day-a-week loan, or even some of some of the animals from Jade's petting zoo she was hoping her sisters would agree to. Children and adults both liked petting zoos, and it had been scientifically proven that exposure to animals could help soothe a person's anxiety and grief. It was yet another way to help people through a tough time.

Speaking of which, this was as good a time as any to tell Zane about her other decision.

"And, Zane?" she said. "I'd like to name the camp Preston's Promise, after my late husband."

He met her gaze with a sad smile. "I like it," he told her. "It's the perfect way to honor his memory."

"Thanks."

She spoke for another minute about some of her other plans for the place, then asked Zane about his own.

"I was thinking we could put up a hedgerow over there," he said, gesturing to their left, "to separate the camp from the watering grounds. Something that will grow fast and dense. Arizona Cypress might be a good solution."

She grinned. "When did you become a gardener?"

He grinned back. "I've been doing some reading."

They both had. Sharing land for two entirely different purposes wasn't going to be nearly as hard as she'd thought. This parcel wasn't huge, but it was big enough for both of them. They really should have thought about a compromise to begin with. But they'd kind of had other things on their minds there at the start. Bringing babies into the world had required the greatest compromise of all, so everything else had flown through the window for a bit. Of course, now that their new family would be living at Zane's house—Sabrina would be moving in next month—the compromises were becoming a bit less overwhelming.

She sighed as she watched the sun disappear over the horizon. The sky was now smudged with the blues and purples of dusk. Zane suggested they return to her house before it got too dark to see what they were doing, especially since they'd ridden to the lakefront on his horse Hawkeye. They could come back here anytime, he reminded her, since they were co-owners.

Co-owners of a lake, she reflected. Much better than being co-parents to their daughters. They'd be parenting their girls together. With all the love a mother and father could give their children.

Life was good, she thought. And it was only going to get better from here.

* * * * *

Don't miss
Fortune's Faux Engagement
by Carrie Nichols,
the next installment in the new continuity
The Fortunes of Texas: Fortune's Secret Children.
On sale October 2024, wherever Harlequin books
and ebooks are sold!